THE BLUE JEAN COLLECTION

THE BLUE JEAN COLLECTION

Thistledown Press Ltd.

Second printing 1994, Third printing 1999,
Fourth printing 2002, Fifth printing 2008

Library and Archives Canada Cataloguing in Publication
Main entry under title:
The Blue jean collection

ISBN 10: 1-894345-64-9
ISBN 13: 978-1-894345-64-4

I. Short stories, Canadian (English).* 2. Young adult fiction, Canadian (English).* 3. Canadianfiction (English) – 20th century.*
PS83291.B484 1992 jC813'.01089283 C92-098111-9
PZ5.B1 1992

Book design by A.M. Forrie
Cover illustration and design by Stéphen Daigle
Printed and bound in Canada
Edited by Peter Carver

Thistledown Press Ltd.
633 Main Street, Saskatoon, Saskatchewan, S7H 0J8
www.thistledownpress.com

Canada Council for the Arts Conseil des Arts du Canada

Canadian Heritage Patrimoine canadien

We acknowledge the support of the Canada Council for the Arts, the Saskatchewan Arts Board, and the Government of Canada through the Book Publishing Industry Development Program for our publishing program.

PUBLISHER'S NOTE

The Blue Jean Collection is the result of Thistledown Press's commitment to publishing short stories for young readers.

In 1991 the press initiated a competition for short stories that would appeal to this audience. The competition was open to writers from across Canada. Two hundred and forty-three stories were submitted by writers from coast to coast. All were presented anonymously for assessment.

An external jury, comprising a children's bookseller, a representative of the Canadian Children's Book Centre and an internationally recognized writer, selected the winning story, "I Am Hilda Burrows" by Sharon Gibson Palermo, and the runner-up, "Saying Goodbye" by Linda Holeman.

The Blue Jean Collection consists of these two and seventeen additional stories selected from the submissions.

Two of those included were not in the final adjudication because they exceeded the competition's guideline for length.

The publisher thanks all the writers who participated in this competition and made it a success. Watch for details of the next competition.

CONTENTS

PREFACE

Fantasy, science fiction, minimalism, realistic and abstract fiction, historical and contemporary fiction – the short stories in this collection display the versatility of styles and voices in short fiction.

What these nineteen stories have in common is that special quality of the short story, the capacity to say much in a few words, to unlock a world by nuance and implication.

What you'll discover here is the power of the short story as a literary form – whether it is in evoking the shocking impact of the Halifax explosion on one lost child, or tracing the tragic deterioration of a much-loved grandmother, or suggesting the delicate nature of unrequited love-at-a-distance, or describing the magical creation of a knight-protector who quickly goes sour.

Within the confines of a few pages – a reading time of only ten or fifteen minutes at most – a character or characters become your intimate friends. A world is explored. The short story writer is a careful miniaturist, each sentence a fine brush stroke. Substantial meaning lies between the lines, thoughts and themes remain unsaid but strongly implied.

Some of the stories in *The Blue Jean Collection* come from established writers whose books are already familiar to thousands of readers. But, just as exciting, more are new voices, writers whose work and careers are freshly begun.

Nineteen short stories from across Canada, nineteen worlds to enter. Welcome to *The Blue Jean Collection.*

Peter Carver
July, 1992

I AM HILDA BURROWS

Sharon Gibson Palermo

Out of the black: dizzied jabs of light, seeping queasiness, cold-wrapped bones. Hilda stirred.

Voices floated through her.

"Nothing's left."

"Worse than death."

"The Germans."

"Wake, child, get up." Someone shook her. "There's another one coming. Get to open ground."

Hilda opened her eyes. There was a black rain. She whimpered. The sickening smell, the voices, the cold – around her as much as in her.

"Don't just lie there!" a voice urged.

Half-alive, half-conscious, no Heaven, no Hell. Stabs of cold, grimy nakedness everywhere. She was breathing filth.

They were the worst visions of all – in her body, not her mind . . . a rolling, thrashing, convulsing through space. And this shivering, uncontrolled. ". . . the death of you . . . the death of you . . . ," the words had come – Mama. And then, violently! Death!

She moved, and pain seared her arm. She screamed.

She was alive! She found a way to sit up. Under the grey smog lay a grey wasteland, churned-up dirt, as if from a tempest, sharp chunks of metal, shards of glass, boards whose nails pierced the air. Beyond them, fires roared.

A child lay, stripped of its clothes, its head twisted askew, one arm missing from where blood flowed out. There were other bodies, writhing, or still. People moved nightmarishly and Hilda gazed. Her good arm wrapped her stomach. She closed her eyes to the dizziness and saw her innards wrench violently, and her body shoot upwards. She opened them.

People hurried single-mindedly toward some destination. Others, disoriented, headed one way, then the other, some sluggish, some bent over, many clutching parts of their bodies, crying, or moaning, or despairingly silent. A woman knelt to the ground, laid down a battered baby, then leaned over it and wailed.

Hilda reached for her quilt but it wasn't there. Hot tears flooded her cheeks. They turned quickly cold, but she noticed none of it. She stood up. She had a notion she must get to the Commons. She began to pick her way along with the single-minded ones. She must get there before the next one came.

Her feet stung. They were bare and bleeding. The ground was covered with rubble, but she managed to avoid the bodies and parts of bodies along the way. She was aware of her feet. Someone covered her shoulders and said, "This here shawl's all I got. There'll be a blanket. Them's that aren't hurt are helpin'. Even some that are. Hold th' arm up, dear." The person lifted it, painfully, to rest against her body on her good arm. "Look out for carts goin' to the Camp Hill. Love! Snap out of it! What's your name?"

Name?

"'Nother one shocked. Hold that arm up till y'get it splinted," the voice said, imperatively. "Keep a lookout for a cart."

She resumed picking her way, aware now of her arm and its throbbing. Sometime later, she passed a man with half a face. It bled sickeningly, but a woman pushed him onward. "There's going to be another one," she urged. "We have to keep moving." But the man sank to the ground. Crying out, the woman begged him to stand, then ran on.

After a time, someone wrapped Hilda in a blanket and pressed arms around her. A breath of warmth seeped through her.

"Mama?" she asked.

"No. I'm not your mother. What's your name?"

"Mama?" There was a face . . . her mind flashed images. Faces – in orange, dancing – no – pausing, fuzzed and grey, then wild suddenly. Familiar faces bombarded into her, out of her.

The person shook her shoulders gently, but pain stabbed her arm. "Try and remember who you are."

Words came. She spoke them, murmuring, "'Come in, Hilda. You're sick. This will be the death of you."

"Is that you? Are you Hilda?"

"I am Hilda Burrows," she said hollowly. The sound of her voice interested her. "I am Hilda Burrows," she said again.

"Burrows," the person repeated, hands firm on her shoulders.

"Hilda Burrows."

"Yes, Hilda. You'll be all right. Your clothes have been blown away."

She looked into his face. He was neither old nor young, kind nor cruel. She was beginning to see: despair, skin touching air, pain. These were real.

"My clothes?"

"Your clothes were blown right off you. Don't worry. It happened to many. You're covered now."

Hilda shook her head. "Colin?" she begged. "Colin and Keith? Where are they? They were right here . . ." She saw the small faces of her brothers, excited, then suddenly – grey? "Aren't they here? Where am I?"

"Near Robie and North, I think. It's hard to tell exactly. Nothing's left." His voice slid away and he looked out past her shoulder.

"Nothing's left?"

"Of this part of Halifax," he said, coming to himself again. "Where do you live?"

"On Hanover Street. I – how did I get here? What happened?" A cold rush through her – she thought she would vomit.

"Hanover Street. It's gone. Everything over there is gone. Burning down now, what's left of it. A place will be found for you after you're cared for. God knows, somehow they'll find clothes and homes and food for everyone!" He wrapped his arms around her. "Try not to panic," he said, then, steadily, "It's important to stay calm. Here comes the hospital cart." The man lifted her up and placed her in it.

"Wait! What happened?" But the man walked on, turning his attention to someone else.

Her eyes travelled past him to the destruction and flames. This was not Hell but some living earth in the midst of Hell. Her cart-mates were maimed and wounded. The blood-stained face of a woman regarded her silently. The woman seemed whole.

"Love," she said, "don't you know? A ship exploded. Two fool ships collided. You seen that one, Belgian Relief, that's been around the past coupla days? And that other one she collided with, that one that caught fire, she was loaded with explosives for Europe."

Hilda gasped: her brothers before her, stomping up the hill to school, turning at the top, eyes wide at the laughing tongues of flame, two blocks down their street, in the harbour. "Hear that cracklin' 'n' poppin'?" Colin exclaimed.

They'd called her to see the excitement. She'd gone out, wrapped in a quilt, fevered with 'flu, wearing only a nightdress and slippers.

Through the door, Mama's skin reflected the spectacle. "You've been sick for a week, Hilda!"

The December air had chilled her. She'd moved to go inside.

Then – Oh, God! It was real – a single blaring, renting blast! The faces vanished.

She huddled more deeply into her blanket. Her feet were bare and torn and under the blanket she was almost entirely naked! Behind her, where she lived, everything was burning. She was weak from 'flu and her head reeled. There'd been a rapid whirling through space . . .

How had she gotten from Hanover Street to near North? What was she remembering? Every bone and tissue within her jerking out – she *thought* she had felt that – jerking to the balloon wall of her skin and, mercifully, jerking back. Somewhere within that instant, her brothers' faces shot away.

She stared at the woman trance-like, trying to remember.

"I am Hilda Burrows," she said, as if protecting herself.

"What happened to you, love?" the woman asked.

Hilda diverted her eyes. She *couldn't* have tornadoed through space, spinning dervishly . . . It was Laura who believed things, ghosts at the foot of her bed, space monsters at the window-pane, jumping into bed with Hilda, saying, "I'll always take care of you!"

The woman persisted, "It's best to talk. The whole city's in this. Silly talk saying there'll be another. Wasn't no German bomb at all. What would they be doing way over here this side of the Atlantic? Enough's going on over there. Weren't no Germans, but a big accident and there won't be another one. Now we gotta help each other. Me and you, we're lucky. Some say people were blown right to bits. Others just died completely whole right where they were, didn't feel nothing. Awfullest thing. Strangest thing."

Hilda kept looking out past everything. "I think I flew," she whispered.

"Yeah?" the woman pressed, startled.

"There was a big hollow space all around. Like a tunnel. Or a funnel sucking me up." She turned to the woman who knew so much. "Is that possible?"

"Love, that's the strangest thing. But that explosion coulda done most anything. Why not funnel you up?"

Hilda pressed her eyes shut. She'd crashed, solidly, with shattering pain, to blackness. And Colin and Keith, and Mama and Papa and Laura?

Mama had gone into the house . . . .

And Papa working at the dockyards, right by where that ship had been. "Lucky Papa!" little Keith said. "Down there right close!"

"No sense worrying no more," the woman went on. "What's done's done. You'll get to the Camp Hill, they'll fix you up, help you find your kin." Her voice changed then, solemn, sorrowful. "That is, if you still got any kin. If any of us got any."

"Oh!" sobbed Hilda suddenly. "Oh, God!" she cried in utter realization. "Is the hospital all right? My sister is a nurse there! Is it standing?"

"Far as I know. That's where they're taking us, love."

"Thank God!" she gasped, pulling both arms to her mouth, but the broken one fell with a sharp stab.

The cart plodded past the devastation and wounded. Hilda was safe now that Laura would cradle her and splint her arm and dab her wounded feet with peroxide. Laura, big sister, imaginative and brave.

The woman undid her high lace boots. She removed them and pulled off two wool socks. Reaching them out to Hilda, she said, "Put these on. Your feet are turning blue, even under all that blood."

Hilda took them and, pulling a sliver of glass from near a toe, she eased them on, naturally, deserving of them.

With slow understanding, she looked to the woman to thank her. Instead, she saw her mother begging her to come in. Her mind pulsed faces, words, "I'll always take care of you."

Suddenly, frantically, awkwardly, she held the blanket about her and, with the same hand, grabbed the cart's edge. She thrust a leg over the side.

"Stop!" someone hollered. "Girl wants out!"

"Miss, what are you doing?" others cried. She paid no heed, but shuffled to the ground. The blanket fell open, exposing her nakedness. Her feet throbbed with a pain she hadn't noticed before. The city was in pain, her family in need. She moved toward the burning North End where her home was.

Wildness took hold. She ran toward the flames nearly half a mile from where she was. Her mind was alert. Her fever still simmered. Laura and Mama were there, in her mind, putting icepacks on her head, trying to pull her out of the heaviest part. She had to reach her family. First, the dockyards, the greatest destruction. Papa could be floating face down in the harbour, or flat dead like the others she'd heard of.

He could be bleeding, missing something – any movement might make it worse.

But was the house burning with Mama inside? What could she do?

Oh! There was Keith not far from her, wandering around, sobs ripping at him, with only one shoe. There were clothes on him. Choking joyously, she hurried closer to wrap him in her blanket and carry him with her . . . but no! She stopped, devastated, and stared at some other child, a deep gash in front of his ear, bits of glass in his hair and head. She moved on. To help him would be a helpless act.

She forgot her feet, though she travelled constantly over sharp debris. The blanket didn't hinder her. Her bad arm was wrapped like a sling, the other arm just under it, hugging her body, closing the blanket tightly around her.

She reached the burning. Flames stopped her advancement. There were no familiar landmarks. There was not a building standing, but piles of ripped houses aflame. The spectacular burning of the ship – distant, beautiful, warming – had leapt to shore to become this blazing inferno. Was there no entry? Could there be no escape?

There was one hope for Papa – that he had been shot to safety as she had been.

So she would go home.

She was frozen before the flames.

Pain and weakness, or fear and confusion, buckled her knees. What was real about her? She should've gone on to the hospital where Laura would prop up her feet and speak in laughing big sister tones . . . .

Soldiers were about, pulling boards from buildings, carrying wounded and dead away from the holocaust. She picked her way slowly along untouched paths, holding her blanket from the edge of the flames, until she came around Fort Needham hill on the harbour side, not far from where her house had been. A soldier stood apart. His face drooped. Sweat streaked black soot down his cheeks. He reached out and pulled gently at a strand of her hair.

"Poor child," he said wearily. "Black, but you're standing, and I don't see any glass in your head." She wiped at her cheek, bringing away soot on whiter fingertips.

"Sir, where's Hanover Street?"

"Nothing left of it, I'm afraid."

"But my mother is in the house."

He drew her into his chest. It was a strange comfort being held by a stranger. When he loosened his hold, she drew away to cold, wet tears. Shocked, she moved more deeply into the maze of paths, nearer to home.

"Don't, Miss," he warned. She continued on and he ran to her, grabbing her shoulder. "Don't! That blanket will go up in a second! And these flames will close in. I'll get you out of here."

From beneath the snap of burning came a moan.

"What are you doing just standing there?" she shouted suddenly, never having ordered anyone in her life. She manoeuvered at the edge of a pile of rubble not yet aflame. Boards and nails and crumbled plaster criss-crossed deeply towards the ground. A sound came from under it.

"Sir! There's someone down there!"

"You sure?"

"Yes! Listen!"

Silently, they perked their hearing above the burning.

"You're right," he whispered, tense and alert. "You'll have to get rid of that blanket and brave the cold for a few minutes. And do just as I tell you so we don't cause anything to fall farther down. Here, careful now, help me with this board."

Underneath her blanket was a shred of underwear held together by a strip of elastic.

Her bosom was newly formed and secret. "Don't look at me," she pleaded, and he wasn't looking. She let the blanket drop. She let her bad arm hang limply, and he turned because he needed her help.

"Good God!" he cried. "First thing is to get you out of here!" He was frantic now as if he had too much to care for at once. He tried putting the blanket around her again, forcing her to support her arm, but she balked. Whoever was under there – maybe Mama or Colin or Keith – whoever, needed help and fire was encroaching.

"I've got a good arm!" she cried, imperative now, and older than she was. "Don't look at me, just tell me what to do."

His face was urgent and gratifying.

"All right. Can you lift the end of this board? It's a heavy one."

Now, with the necessity of the moment, her suffering came over her. To give in! To give up! But she had done nothing yet! She could flee. To help one other person flee also!

The broken arm was not part of her. She worked the other hand around the end of a long piece of wood. Gingerly and together, she and the soldier carried away parts of the fallen house. Below, moans alerted them to life, but no one answered their calls of hope. Could it be one of the Burrows? Hilda pressed on, calling down now and again, "Mama? Colin?"

Every pain, every moment, screamed. Her body fevered deeply and the bitter ice of skin wrapped her. She was pierced with fear and shame, yet heat from the flames blanketed her shoulders. The shock into nothingness had reversed itself. Something was pushing her on, but it could be neither Colin nor Keith nor Mama down below. This was the wrong part of the hill.

She hardened herself against what she might find.

"I am Hilda Burrows," she murmured once.

There were no words between her and the soldier other than, "this board, now," or "that one," spoken by him who had not looked at her again.

Finally, they reached a child who had given up whimpering. His legs were crushed and some fingers severed under a fallen beam. Hilda found a spot for her knees and bent toward him. He looked into her eyes and she knew he was someone's brother. His face was blue with cold. She wrapped her good arm under him, and bending further, pulled them towards each other, burying his face in her chest, feeling his slowly pulsing body.

SAYING GOOD-BYE

Linda Holeman

This is the first summer I've been to the Island without my dad. It's also the first summer that I've been alive and he hasn't.

Sitting in my aunt and uncle's house, I watch Delia stuff a thick slice of warm, home-made bread into her mouth, then chew slowly, her front teeth showing, staring at the gently smiling face of Jesus on the wall in front of her.

The ancient calendar is thumbtacked to the wallpaper of golden teapots and pink and green daisies; the year at the bottom of the curling, yellowed page is so colourless it's hard to read. Nineteen seventy-something, three or eight. Over Jesus' halo the faded words "And Ye Shall Be Touched By Him" are followed by a smaller, even more faded message – "A Prayer from the Ladies of St. Winifred Chapter." The calendar has hung on the wall behind the table as long as I can remember – ever since I was a little kid and had started coming to the Island with my dad. Even though everything else has changed, the calendar is still there.

With a noisy swallow, Delia reaches for the long bread knife and starts to carefully saw through the crumbling loaf.

"Cut a piece for Liza," Auntie Yvonne says, love shining from her glittering black eyes as she looks at Delia, her youngest child, the only one left at home now. Then her gaze moves reluctantly to me.

"Liza could use another slice. We don't want your mother thinking we didn't feed you, do we?"

I shake my head. Delia ignores her mother and, with the same knife, spreads a huge blob of butter over the soft surface of her bread, then, looking at me, licks the last creamy smears off the knife, her quick pointed tongue caressing the sharp edge.

"Pass the jam," she says around the blade.

"The strawberry or the chokecherry?"

"Strawberry."

"Delia, didn't you hear me?" Auntie Yvonne says, wiping her wet hands on a tea towel and pushing back a strand of shiny black and dull grey hair that had come loose from the thick ponytail. The veins on the backs of her strong brown hands are raised and ropey as she starts to slice through the loaf with a clean knife.

"It's okay, Auntie. I'm not hungry." I smile to show that I don't mind Delia being rude.

My aunt looks at me, then suddenly her lips begin moving, trembling against each other the way rose petals do when a summer breeze blows up. Covering her mouth with her hand, she quickly turns back to the sink.

I know why she's crying. It still happens to my mom sometimes. Everyone's always said that my smile is exactly like my dad's. I try to remember, but sometimes I just forget and smile right at the people who loved him most.

The Island was his home. He grew up here, with his parents and his big sister Yvonne, on this tiny, tree-covered bump right in the middle of Lake Winnipeg. There are only fourteen houses scattered between stands of scrawny jack pine and whispering aspen and poplar, and just about everyone is related in some way.

Mostly older people live on the Island now; their kids usually go down to the city – or maybe to Riverton or Selkirk – to look for jobs. They can't make enough money fishing any more.

Besides Delia, there's just Billy Linklater's kids, a whole bunch of them. Ronette's the oldest, the same age as Delia and me. Delia can't wait to leave; she says in another year, as soon as she's sixteen, she's going down to stay with her cousin Willa, who rents a house in Lockport and has a job at the Crazee Fun Water Slide in summer and at the Lockport Hotel in the winter.

The Island's real name is Loon Island, but no one calls it that any more, not since my dad was a baby and all the kids started coming home from the school on the mainland saying that the white kids called them Loonies. My dad used to laugh about that story, saying no one would mind being called a Loonie now that it means money. Back then it just meant crazy.

The Island feels different without my dad. When we came for our three weeks every summer, just the two of us, we'd stay in the little fishing shack right down by the water, curling up in sleeping bags on musty blown-up air mattresses. But we'd eat up at the house with Auntie Yvonne and Uncle Mort and whatever kids were around that year. Every night, before we went to sleep, Dad and I would lie on our backs in the long sweet grass beside the shack and watch the sky, and he'd point out the constellations, and tell me the old Ojibwa legends, and what the

Island was like when he was a boy, and stories about me as a baby.

My mom never came with us. She said she'd had a taste of island living the summer she met my dad, and she'd rather relax in the city, thank you very much. She hadn't been back since the summer they'd met, when she came up as a university student on a youth grant, to help record data for the Fisheries. My dad said she was like a snow angel, with her long white-blonde hair and pink skin, and he was so enchanted with her that he gave his boat and all his fishing gear to Delia's oldest brother and followed Mom back to the city, got a job in construction, and married her.

This summer was my mom's idea. I didn't want to come, but she said it would make me feel less lonely for Dad, remembering all the good times with him, when he was big and brown, with a laugh that echoed across the water at night, not the sad, yellow stranger in a hospital gown that he was for most of my thirteenth year and part of my fourteenth.

And you have a job to do there, she'd said with a stern look, as if I could ever forget what my dad had asked me to do.

So far the whole week has been a total disaster. Without Dad there doesn't seem to be anything to do, and I feel like a stranger, a tall, skinny girl with short blonde hair and narrow black eyes.

I don't have to stay any longer than I want; someone goes across the lake every day before ten. All I have to do is show up at the big dock with my backpack, get a lift to the mainland, walk the three blocks to the Bun's Up Bakery where the bus stops, and phone my mom to meet me at the bus station at 6:45. Each day I think that today's the day I'll do what I came to do, but then I lose my nerve.

Auntie Yvonne has tried hard to make me feel welcome, but Delia is another story; she's never liked me, even when we were both dumb little kids. She'd act all sweet and friendly when Dad was around, but as soon as he'd go off to visit his old buddies she'd turn nasty, taking me to parts of the island I didn't recognize and then running away and leaving me, or telling me scary stories about vicious island bears or the lady with a face like an old map that lived in a tiny log house down near the water.

Even though Delia can't scare me any more, she still finds ways to make me feel stupid.

After her third piece of bread and jam, we go out to sit on the roof of the fishing shack, looking at the lake. After a while Ronette comes by and climbs up to join us. It's hot, so hot that even the flies seem to be buzzing slower than usual.

"Want to go swimming later?" Ronette asks. She's pretty nice – probably because she's the oldest and used to sharing everything, including her mother's attention.

"Sure," I say.

"How about you, Delia?" Ronette asks, poking Delia's shoulder.

Delia jerks away from the jabbing finger. "Cut it out, Ronnie. I'll think about it." She pulls a folded *Teen Star* magazine out from the back pocket of her shorts. "Hey, did you see the latest picture of Wicked Willie?" She opens the magazine and hands it to Ronette.

"Cute," says Ronette, looking at the smudged sheet, then passes it to me. I glance down at the blurry photo of the band and give it back to Delia.

"So, don't you think the lead guitarist is something?" she asks me.

"Yeah, he's okay," I say. I've never been into heavy metal.

Delia won't let it drop. "I can't believe you don't just DIE when you look at him. I mean, those lips! I bet he's a fabulous kisser. Don't you think he'd be a good kisser, Liza?"

I study a leaf stuck to the side of my bare foot. "I guess," I say casually.

Hearing the smirk in Delia's voice, I look up.

"She GUESSES so, Ronnette." She turns towards me again. "I GUESS you wouldn't know, would you, Liza? You've never even kissed a guy, have you?"

I pick the leaf off, ordering my cheeks and neck not to turn that horrible dull red that shouts to everyone how I'm feeling. I inherited my dad's eyes and smile, but my mom's hair and skin.

"If I haven't kissed anyone, Delia – and I'm not saying I haven't –" I said, pausing for effect and thinking about Danny Mitchell's embarrassing attempt in May after the block party, "it's because I haven't felt like it." I didn't add that even when I have felt like kissing someone, for example Danny's best friend Bryan, they don't always pick up on that feeling.

"Don't make me laugh," Delia shrieked, then proceeded to do so, throwing back her head and letting out a bray that sent a sparrow perched on the eave flapping straight up in alarm. "Princess Liza hasn't felt like kissing anyone. Pretty weird for a fourteen-year-old, eh Ronette? Not to feel like kissing a boy? Oh-oh," she kept on, moving away from me, her bottom scraping across the old shingles and sending tiny particles of gravel rolling down the roof, "maybe she's the type that isn't interested in boys at all. Oh-oh," she repeated, giggling and fluttering her eyelashes at me.

Ronette stood up suddenly, her knees bent on the steep incline, and shielded her eyes with her arm as she looked out at the grey-green water. "Looks like Douglas is coming in. Let's go see if he brought the mail." She leapt off the low roof, landing in the grass with a muffled thud.

Delia got to her feet, supporting herself with one hand as she cautiously made her way to the edge, then jumped off heavily.

"Come on, Liza," Ronette called up. "Walk down with us." I looked down into her round face and smiled gratefully.

"No thanks, Ronette. You go on. I'm going to stay here for a while. If it doesn't cool off I'll meet you at the dock later for a swim."

I don't go for a swim. Instead, I take a long walk up to North Point, past the caved-in Anglican church with four broken pews still inside. I automatically start to hold my breath as I get close to the tiny graveyard a hundred meters from the church, then blow it out with an irritated noisy whistle. I'm too old to believe in that junk Delia told me when we were seven or eight.

I stop and look at the three rows of tilting wooden crosses inside the peeling white picket fence. No one's been buried here for at least twenty years, Auntie Yvonne told me, not since the big new church was built on the mainland and the minister stopped coming out. The mainland cemetery holds the Island people now.

As a soft, cool draft blows up from the water, I think, for at least the hundredth time, about the container in my battered old green backpack, then turn and walk back to the house.

Later, after supper, when all that's left of the sun is a thin streak of shell pink in the sky over the water, I ask Auntie Yvonne for a sleeping bag. She just nods, and when she hands it to me, squeezes my shoulder so hard it hurts. Her eyes look like they want to say something, but her mouth stays a straight, sealed line. Delia looks up from the couch, where she's flipping through another magazine, and for once even she doesn't say anything, just puts her head down and starts flicking the pages faster.

I spread the sleeping bag beside the fishing shack and sit cross-legged on it. I wait, for maybe ten minutes or maybe an hour, until the sky has turned from black felt to a bold, gloriously sparkling blanket, and the lake's night wind is blowing with quiet persistence. Then from inside my sweat-shirt I pull out the small metal canister. Its lightness still surprises me. I unscrew the lid, and look down at the ashes.

Standing up, I start giving the canister small shakes, watching as the ashes float up and are carried away. When the can is empty, I lie down on the sleeping bag and stare up into the sky, waiting. The wind blows my hair against my cheek, and suddenly the summer smell of the water and grass combine in an almost unbearable sweetness. I take a deep breath, and for the first time in a long, long while, feel my eyes start to close in that easy, perfect way that you know means you'll slide into sleep peacefully, without remembering what you don't want to remember and worrying about things that make you so tired that sleep won't come.

I think about the ride home tomorrow, and how I'll buy two boxes of Junior Mints for the trip, and about the feeling of my mom's arms around me as I step off the bus.

THE RINK

R.P. MacIntyre

The trouble with being an older brother is you got to drag your younger brother everywhere you go. That, and keep him covered in band-aids ever time he scrapes himself, which is about every ten seconds. He loves band-aids.

So just when stuff starts getting exciting and you're with your friends, there he is, twenty steps behind you, yelling, "Hey! Wait for me!" That's the way it usually is.

It's a couple of years ago on Hallowe'en, and as per usual I'm supposed to be taking my five-year-old brother Cory trick-or-treating, and really I am, but on the way home we run into some of my friends.

Shane, who is a kind of leader of our gang, has a neat idea. He also has a pellet gun. He says he found it, but with Shane you never know. Anyway, he wants to go over to old man Givens' house and maybe pop out a few windows.

Old man Givens was the principal at our school till he retired last year. Givens the Geezer we called him and he was about as mean as you can be. I never actually saw him give the strap because they don't allow that any more, but they said he used to use half a meter of a special, thick black licorice because it didn't leave any marks. And then he'd sort of eat it on the school grounds, in front of everybody. He never used to yell. He didn't need to. All he did was whisper and everyone listened. So anyway, I really want to go with Shane and the gang, but Cory is with me, and everything I do when Cory is around, my Mom finds out about. I mean, Cory is basically a nice kid but he has a mouth as big as a bathtub. So I send him home and promise that if he says a word to Mom, I'll eat all his Hallowe'en candy.

We go over to Givens the Geezer's house and park ourselves behind some bushes. Cam and Jerry have two bars of soap and work over Geezer's car. We try not to laugh too loud. Donny, another friend, has a dozen eggs. He gives a couple to me. We time it so that as Shane shoots his gun, Donny and I fire the eggs through the broken window.

On the count of three we do it, and it works like crazy! Shane's gun doesn't actually make a hole big enough for the eggs to go through. They slobber all over the window instead and it's really just as good. We run like mad! We can hear alarms going off.

It's not even an hour later when I get home. But I hardly walk through the door and I can tell that Bathtub Mouth has said something to Mom and Dad. I look at him and he says, "I told them you were going to take my candy if I said."

Cory gets the candy. I get in trouble, big time.

When it's all over, the police find that Shane's gun is hotter than a pancake, and he actually goes to Wilbur Hall, a place for jaydees. The rest of us are on some kind of probation where we have to work for people doing odd jobs.

Guess where I have to work? You got it – Geezer Givens'.

I guess I deserve every minute of it, but to tell you the truth, it's not as bad as I thought it would be. He taught science at school and is a real electronics nut. He has all these gadgets and doodads, remote this and automatic that, half of which don't work but which of course he's trying to fix. I have to work for three hours a week for ten weeks, just about till Christmas. The kind of stuff I do is help him clean the attic and the garage, shovel his walks, and a bunch of other odd jobs no one would ever normally do, like washing the basement ceiling.

So far the strangest thing I help him with is this intercom he has hooked up from his house to the garage. He wants to check and see if it's working. He says it's to hear the garage door opening. I thought they were for talking through. I mean, who's he going to talk to – himself? Anyway, it works.

I've been there three or four weeks and I've been in every room in his house, except one. This one has its door closed all the time. Then, one day, I find out something I wish I didn't know.

"Come here, Jason," he says.

"Yeah?"

He opens the door and says, "I've been putting this off for months. I guess I should clean it up." In the room is all kinds of sewing stuff, pictures on the walls that look hand-painted, and all kinds of knick-knacky stuff. It's quite a mess. "My wife's," he says.

"I didn't know you were married." You never think of your ex-principal as being married.

"She passed away in August," he says. "My boy wanted to clean it after the funeral, but I wouldn't let him."

"I didn't know you had kids." I can be pretty stupid sometimes.

He takes a photograph that's above the sewing machine. It's got a man and a woman and a little baby in it. The man is holding the baby.

"This is my boy Michael. Lives in Toronto. That's my grandson, Bradley. He's six now. And that's Judy," he says pointing at the picture. "They're coming for Christmas. I'll need the room."

He gives me a package of garbage bags and says, "Put as much of this in these as you can." I notice his hand is shaking. "Take them out to the garage."

He turns and walks away. Fast. He doesn't want me to see the tears starting in his eyes. But I see them anyway.

The next week it has definitely turned colder and that first mat of snow hides the frozen dirt. You know what I mean, where you kick a lump you think is snow but you just about break your foot.

Anyway, Mr. Givens and I are in his backyard where his garden used to be. There's still dangly frozen tomato plants sticking up and other stuff he wants cleared out. He paces off a square in the snow and says, "Get this as level and clean as you can. This is where it's going."

"What?" I ask.

"The rink," he says. "For my grandson, for Christmas."

I never made a rink before, so I get kind of excited about it and I tell Mom and Dad. Cory, who is big into hockey, thinks this is the cat's meow. He's never *seen* anyone make a rink before and wants to come and watch. I figure it's not going to hurt anyone, so in a couple of days I take him along to Mr. Givens'.

Mr. Givens is kind of surprised to see me because I'm not *supposed* to be there for another four days. But I tell him my little brother wants to watch us make the rink, and he gets all cheerful, and even though he's in the middle of watching a hockey game on TV, he gets dressed, hauls the hose outside, and we start putting water where the rink will be.

Mr. Givens has already put little boards around it and in a few minutes, after the water has soaked through the snow, it looks like a box of ugly cold slushy mud. I personally don't see how this is going to be a rink of any kind, but Cory likes the steam going up and chirps at

Mr. Givens, asking a zillion questions, like little kids do. Bathtub Mouth.

"Can I skate on it?" asks Cory.

"Sure you can," says Mr. Givens, "but the first one to skate on it is going to be my grandson, Brad. You'll like him. He's just about your age."

"When's he coming?" asks Cory.

"He'll be here for Christmas," says Mr. Givens.

"That's a long time," says Cory.

"Not as long as you think," says Mr. Givens. "Well, that should do her for now. All we can do is seal it tonight."

"What's sealing?" asks Cory.

"To keep the water from leaking out. Sort of like a band-aid stops bleeding," says Mr. Givens.

The questions go on and on, while we put the hose away, while Mr. Givens gives us hot chocolate, in fact until we leave. When we get out of the house and are on our way home, Cory is as quiet as he was noisy at Mr. Givens'. Too quiet.

"What's the matter?" I ask.

"Is sealing really like a band-aid to stop bleeding?"

That's what he asks me, honest. Kids.

Over the next few weeks Cory and I go over to Mr. Givens' a lot. Sometimes I pull him over in the sleigh when the snow is fresh, before people get their walks cleared. It's fun. But when the walks are cleared, we walk. It's only a couple of blocks.

The rink actually starts looking like a rink the closer we get to Christmas, and we're actually starting to be friends, especially Mr. Givens and Cory. But the closer Christmas comes, the more edgy Mr. Givens gets. Even Cory notices it. And being Bathtub Mouth, he asks. "What's the matter, Mr. Givens?"

Mr. Givens is incredibly patient with Cory's questions. He always answers. It would drive me nuts.

"Well, this is the first Christmas without Mrs. Givens, Cory. It just makes me a little sad, that's all."

"Oh," says Cory. He thinks about it for a second, then asks, "Why does that make you sad?"

I can't believe he asks that! That is not the kind of question you ask somebody and expect an answer. It's too personal. But, you guessed it, Mr. Givens answers.

"Well, me and my son tend to argue a bit, and Mrs. Givens was always there to . . ." – he looks for words – "...to keep us from hurting each other too bad. To stop the bleeding."

"Like a band-aid," says Cory.

"That's right," chuckles Mr. Givens, "Mrs. Givens was like a band-aid."

"She'd seal things."

"She sure would."

When we get outside, I give Bathtub Mouth heck for getting so personal.

"Don't call me Bathtub Mouth," he says.

"Well then, don't ask such stupid questions."

"If I don't ask, how am I going to know?" says Cory.

I got to admit, for a question, it's a pretty good answer. It shuts me up anyway. It also makes me forget the sleigh.

Neither of us remember the sleigh till a couple of days later when it snows again. Christmas holidays have started and we trudge through the snow, past all the lit houses, till we get to Mr. Givens'. We were going to scrape the rink and give it one more flood before Mr. Givens' grandson arrives.

But when we get there, the house is dark. It's like a black hole in the block, next to all the other houses. Our sleigh is nowhere in sight.

Mr. Givens must have put it in the garage, or maybe in the back of the house.

We go around the back and there is no sled, but the rink is freshly scraped and flooded. The moonlight shines off it like a knife. It's almost spooky, as if something's dead. Cory wants to slide on it, but I say, "No. It's for his grandson first."

We get half a block away when a car pulls into Mr. Givens' driveway. It's them, Mr. Givens, his son and family. They get out of the car. In the clear air we can hear them like they're next to us and Mr. Givens says, "Watch this!" He waves his arms and all of a sudden, his house lights up like a Christmas tree. Spelled out in letters of light is "Welcome Judy, Michael and Brad!! Merry Christmas."

"Oh, that's sweet," says a woman I guess is Judy.

"Very nice, Dad," says Michael.

"Can we go in?" says grandson Bradley. "I'm cold."

Cory wants to go back and get the sleigh. But I tell him we should wait till tomorrow.

It's Christmas Eve. Cory and I trek over to Mr. Givens'. We go to the door. I'm just about to push the doorbell, when I stop. I can hear yelling in the house. I look at Cory. He can hear it too.

Sometimes, with your brother, you know exactly what each other is thinking, and right now we're both thinking about what Mr. Givens said, about his wife not being there. And how she stopped the fighting.

I turn to go but Cory pushes the doorbell. The yelling stops. Mr. Givens answers the door.

"What do you want?" he says. His face is red.

"Our sleigh," I manage to say.

"In the garage," he says, and closes the door.

A second later we hear the garage door rumble open. We go in and there, leaning up against the far wall, is the sleigh. Right next to it is the intercom I helped test weeks ago. I know it works. Cory looks at me with question marks in his eyes. I turn it on. We listen.

"I don't care if you flooded from here to Calgary . . ." Michael.

"I don't want to go skating. I hate it outside." Brad.

"If Brad doesn't want to go skating, he doesn't have to go skating!" Michael.

"Fine, get the hell out then!" Mr. Givens.

We hear a door slam and through the window we see Mr. Givens heading towards the garage. Cory and I dive behind the car.

"Where's he going?" Judy says over the intercom.

"I don't know." Michael.

"Can't you two get along?" Judy.

Mr. Givens is in the garage by now, with no coat. He doesn't see us.

"Shut up!" he yells at the intercom. It goes silent.

He goes to the wood stacked against the wall. He picks up an ax. Cory and I freeze, if you can freeze even more when you're already frozen.

He goes outside, but instead of going back to the house, he goes to the backyard. Cory runs after him.

"Mr. Givens!" he's saying, "Mr. Givens!"

I follow Cory. Mr. Givens is at the rink. He's chopping at it with the ax. He is like a madman. Chips of ice are flying everywhere, splinters of board.

"Mr. Givens, don't!" Cory is yelling. "Mr. Givens!"

Mr. Givens stops. He is sweating and breathing hard.

"Why are you doing that to the ice?" asks Cory.

By now Mr. Givens' son Michael is there, and so is Judy, his wife.

"Dad, stop – come on in," Michael says. He tries to take the ax.

"Leave me alone," says Mr. Givens.

"Are you looking for the seal, Mr. Givens? Remember the first night when we sealed it?" asks Cory.

Mr. Givens' hand relaxes, the ax falls. His eyes turn to Cory. Then he crumbles to the ice with his hands over his face. He starts crying like a baby. "Yes, yes," he says, "I'm looking for the seal."

"What's he talking about? Dad, what are you talking about? Are you okay?" asks Michael. He puts his hand on his father's back.

"He misses your mom," Cory says. "He said she kept you from fighting. You shouldn't fight on Christmas."

"I'm sorry, Dad. I miss her too," says Michael, the son. He crouches down beside Mr. Givens and talks real slow, like he's looking for the right words. "It's a beautiful rink, Dad. I just can't make Brad skate on it. He's not me. When you made all those rinks for me, when I was a kid, those were the best days of our lives. We never fought, we just played. But then I got too big for it. And we didn't play any more. We needed Mom, we *used* Mom to keep us from fighting. We got to learn to do it alone, Dad."

Mr. Givens lifts his head. He straightens up, still on his knees, on the ice. He looks up at the stars.

"I love you, Dad," says Michael. And they hug. Right there on the rink.

We've all been standing around like icicles, pointy end up. We look at each other, kind of embarrassed, but feeling sad and happy all at the same time.

"Can I skate on the rink now, Mr. Givens?" Cory asks.

Mr. Givens smiles through his tears. "It's all yours," he says.

"Yours too," says Cory. "Maybe Brad will come out when he sees me skating. We'll have to fix the holes though."

"Yes, we will."

He's a neat kid, Cory. I decide then and there I won't call him Bathtub Mouth any more.

Soon after, we wish them a Merry Christmas and head home. We forget the sleigh again, but it doesn't matter. We'll be back.

MISSING

Judith Wright

Sam knew it was her fault that the pup went missing. The pup was outside with her when she was flooding the garden. She was priming the ground in case there was a hard freeze in the night. The pup was with her, gnawing on an old bone by the tool shed. Sam wasn't paying any attention to her; she was thinking about her skating rink.

It all depended on the weather. Sam needed a head start. She was going to learn how to skate if it killed her this winter. No more clinging to the boards, no more celery-ankles, no more wobbly wipe-outs. She pictured herself weaving long risky twists, watching the world glide towards her in elegant slow motion. In her mind she wore a pair of Peggy Fleming figure skates – not her mother's old floppy ones stuffed with newspaper.

Sam looked up at the wintry sky and thought of all the things she wanted. Like a ten-speed bike and a monsoon jacket for spring, and living in a hot foreign country someday. With her, wishing was always mixed up with the weather. In winter she'd picture a summer day – her dad and her setting fence posts, the wind in the grass and the grasshoppers singing. Come summer, maybe she'd be sitting on the roof of the shed, breathing tarred shingles and roasting her backside, thinking about this skating rink.

The afternoon Kara disappeared the temperature was a few degrees above freezing. The yard and the fields – even the shivery little grove of aspens to the south – were wind-still.

Kara still hadn't showed up by the time Sam's mom got home. Rebecca was crabby – she had worked a double shift at the service station. Kita, Kara's mother, didn't seem too worried, but Rebecca kept going to the door to ring the school bell.

"KAA RAAAH!" Ding-da-ding, ding.

Rebecca used the old school bell to call Sam and the dogs. Sam could hear the bell all the way down by the railroad tracks. But Kara didn't hear it. At least she didn't come.

"How could you forget?" Rebecca snapped at Sam. "She's too little to know where home is."

"I dunno," Sam said. "I just forgot."

"Forgot!" Rebecca chewed her lip so that her broken tooth showed. "I oughta leave *you* outside, oughta to make *you* go without supper – maybe that'd jog your memory next time."

After supper Sam's mom said she was going to take the bell and the truck up the highway a ways.

"You want me to come?" Sam asked.

But Rebecca was already in her parka and overalls. "You got homework," she said. "If Kara comes back, you flash the yard light. Think you can handle that?"

When she was gone, Sam got out her book. The book was called *Kidnapped,* by Robert Louis Stevenson. It was one of her favourites, all about this fellow named Davie Balfour who went chasing after his inheritance. The language was difficult. Some parts were so baffling whole sentences stuck in her head. Sam turned a page and began to read.

It was a dark night, with a few stars down low, and as I stood just outside the door, I heard a hollow moaning of wind far off among the hills. I said to myself there was something thundery and changeful in the weather.

"KAAARAAA.... KAARRRAHHH."

Sam frowned and tried to concentrate, but all she could think about was the pup. About all the things she could get into, all the dangers out there. The highway and the railroad tracks. Their dogs were always running away.

I heard a hollow moaning of wind far off among the hills.

She could hear the tar paper flapping against the side of the house. The school bell sounded tin-silvery, far off and lonesome. Rebecca was out there, hollering her lungs out at the wind. She'd probably stop at all the farmhouses; she'd pound on all the doors. Their neighbours would say: it's that crazy Link woman, looking for her dog again.

The following morning the temperature was five below zero. The sky was grey and threatening snow.

"She might have got hit by the train," Rebecca said. She and Sam walked the railroad tracks, scouting both sides of the cinder bed. Their boots crunched the gravel, their breath fogged the air. Rebecca walked ahead of Sam on the ties.

There was a splotch of something on the back of her jacket.

Sam wondered if Rebecca had worn that jacket to her parent-teacher interview. She remembered a line from her book.

Be soople, Davie, in things immaterial.

"What's 'soople,' Ma?"

"You're supposed to be looking," Rebecca said.

"What's immaterial?"

"Not material. The way we live."

"How do we live?"

"Not like other folks," Rebecca said.

Sam could have told her that. Other mothers didn't keep their kids home from school to look for a runaway dog. Other mothers didn't say things like: "The only worthwhile thing my old man left me when he took off was an Alaskan malamute."

"I should have knocked her off when she was born," Rebecca said. "You just get attached. I should have drowned her in a sack, like I said."

Sam knew Rebecca didn't mean it. Rebecca's meanness was just a habit. Like a sickness, it came from somewhere else. It poisoned the air and made everyone around her sick. It made people run away, just like the dogs ran away. Sam remembered the night her dad hit Rebecca with the dog leash. The choke chain flew off and broke Rebecca's tooth. That tooth scared people. Sometimes it scared her.

"You just get attached," Rebecca said. "That's the problem. Getting attached."

Sam listened to Rebecca's skidoo boots thump along the railroad ties. She thought of a line in her book:

Bear ye this in mind, that, though gentle born ye have a country rearing. Dinnae shame us.

Later on that afternoon Rebecca came up with the idea of Patterson's Indian. A neighbour of theirs hired the Indian for odd jobs one summer. The Indian drove his pickup past their place every day. Sam had seen him stopped on the road a couple of times. Once she saw him sitting on the running board, petting Kita. "Fine-looking dog," he said. "Siberian husky?"

He had a magnificent hawk nose. He was a tall, swarthy fellow. He seemed friendly enough. And Kita liked him – which was unusual. She was leery of strangers.

"She a sledder?" he asked.

"Bred for racing," Sam said.

"Looks a little bit heavy."

"She's going to have pups."

Sam knew Rebecca would be mad. She didn't like anyone to know their business. About a week after Kita gave birth to Kara, the Indian knocked on their door. He asked if they had any pups for sale.

"He looked like he didn't have a pot to what-not in," Rebecca said now. "I bet he took her."

She got on the phone to their neighbour, Patterson. As usual, she got straight to the point, no neighbourly small talk.

"Never mind why I want to know," she said. "Where's the joker live?" When she hung up the phone she told Sam, "Get your things on. We're going to town."

It was about five o'clock when they reached town and found the right neighbourhood. "Fifteen, number fifteen... keep your eyes peeled," Rebecca mumbled.

Sam felt like Davie Balfour, approaching the house of Shaws. Number 15 was ordinary-looking enough, no shabbier than their own house, but the late afternoon light made the street sinister. Rebecca parked a few houses down.

"What are you gonna do, Ma?" Sam asked.

"You wait here. If I'm not back in twenty minutes you better call the cops."

"You can't just barge in and say 'you stole our dog,' Ma!"

"Look," Rebecca said. "It's just you and me, right? Nobody's gonna do things for us."

Rebecca wore a yellow toque that said Big Cat. Her face, in the streetlight, looked haggard and pained. She was baggy and blue under the eyes. For a moment Sam felt sorry for her mother. She curled her cold hands in her jacket sleeves and said nothing.

"I'm just gonna take a peek in the backyard," Rebecca said. She pulled her toque down low over her ears. When she laughed her broken tooth flashed.

Sam slid down in her seat. A feeling of disgrace knotted her gut. Why couldn't Rebecca be like other mothers? Why couldn't she have a normal family? No wonder Rebecca's boyfriends never hung around for long. No wonder her dad had run away.

She stared at the houses on the street, at the little squares of light patching the lawns. Furnace smoke drifted from the chimneys. A few snowflakes started to fall. Inside, she expected folks were sitting down to supper. It was getting cold in the truck. She buried her face in Kita's thick fur. Kita was twitchy. Her wet nose smudged the window. Kita was more worried about Rebecca than she was about her pup.

Sam studied the snowflakes that stuck to the windshield and thought about her skating rink. She started to wish for all those impossible things. She wanted the sky to snow and snow, to cover things up, to hide her.

A few minutes later Rebecca was hurrying along towards the truck.

"Well," Sam said when she got in. "Can we go now?"

"There were kennels," Rebecca panted. "I saw two different kinds of paw prints."

"Aw, Ma!" Sam groaned.

They parked the truck in the alley and took Kita with them. Sam felt like a criminal creeping past the garbage cans and backyard fences.

"Okay, it's this one." Rebecca hoisted her up the fence. "See the kennels? See any dogs? Can you reach the latch?"

Sam groaned, her ribs felt like they were breaking as she dangled over the fence. Kita was whining and eager.

"Is it locked?" Rebecca whispered. "Hurry up. What's the matter?"

The gate swung open. They crept into the backyard. Sam was sweating in her parka. She saw someone peep out the lighted window.

"Ma! What are you gonna do?"

"Watch me," Rebecca said. She rapped at the back door. The aluminum door boomed like thunder.

Sam closed her eyes.

There was something thundery and changeful in the weather and I knew little of what a vast importance that should prove to me before the evening passed . . .

She heard the door open. She expected a shepherd and a Doberman to come howling out.

"Yes?"

A woman stood on the porch, balancing a baby on her hip.

"Sorry to bother you," Rebecca started. "It's your husband I want."

Dinnae shame us, Ma. Sam held her breath.

"You must mean Jake, my brother. He's out. What can I do for you?" the woman asked.

Rebecca eyed the baby. "Mind if I step in? I can leave the dog outside with her."

The woman waved all three of them inside. "You looking for a worker?" she asked.

"It's about the dog."

Sam thought: she'll do it. She'll shame us both. And this poor woman. She stared at the dark-eyed baby.

"Are they around, the dogs?" Rebecca asked. "Just the two, you say?"

"You buying or selling?" the woman asked. "I don't think he'll sell."

Just then the back door burst open. Sam let out a yelp. Two male huskies hurled into the kitchen.

Kita leapt up, arched her hackles and stood stiff. She started to wag her tail. The Indian stood on the porch, thumping snow from his boots.

"Jake," the woman said. "Somebody to see you. Don't think we need another dog around," she said to Rebecca, "but you can ask him. He's a fool for dogs."

Rebecca was on her knees running her hands through the huskies' heavy manes. "So am I," she said. "So am I."

Sam would always remember the night in the Indian's kitchen. As she wobbled around the skating rink, she thought of Jake Proudfoot and her mother. She thought about her dad. She thought about the pup, still missing, never found. Weaving long risky twists on the ice, she remembered: *There was something thundery and changeful in the weather.*

MIRRORS

Julie Johnston

When my sisters got back they started arguing about when, exactly, we sold our house. Pat said it wasn't that long ago and Jennie said it was ages.

"Two years ago," I said, "almost to the day." They just looked at me and I know what they were thinking. Right, this spaceman, they were thinking. How would he remember? Come visit our galaxy sometime when you can't stay. And leave your weapons at home.

"I remember it, " I said. "Ask Aunt Bernice, if you don't believe me."

My sisters are older than I am and exist as a unit. Most of the time, I think, I only inhabit the fringes of their lives (they never seem to see me), although I consider them very much a part of my own. If they go out at night, for example, I don't fall asleep until I hear them safely back home and giggling. They used to call me 'the Necessary Evil.' They stopped, though, when the world began to fall apart and I started falling off the edge. My sisters have a certain degree of sensitivity.

When it comes to thinking about the past, sometimes I don't know whether what I remember happened in their lives or in mine. They're always telling stories about the past and I always want to see myself in every one of them. Except for this one, the one they are possibly too sensitive to talk about openly.

For a while, I wasn't absolutely certain I was the one who found the gun in my father's bureau drawer under his linen handkerchiefs just after he died. I remember other things, like my mother with her eyes all bright and two little red splotches at the top edges of her cheeks telling people he was on the mend, when the doctor had just told us, sadly, that he wouldn't last through the week. I remember feeling as if I was going through a bad dream, one where you open the cellar door onto pitch dark and you know you have to go down stairs, and suddenly there are no stairs and you step into nothing. Only I was awake, so I couldn't turn on the light or drink a glass of cold water to make it go away.

When there's nothing under you, no base, you don't think clearly. We all knew the gun was there; it was to scare away burglars, but we never had burglars. We didn't even know if it was loaded. None of us had ever fired a gun. Now, two years later, I can picture it nestled in its black, satin-lined case, so small, like something you'd see in a joke shop. A bang-bang-you're-dead type of thing with a red flag popping out.

I don't remember the next part. Somehow it got into my pants pocket because it was there at the funeral home when we had what they call "the wake." A kind of twisted term, I think, but in our case, as it turned out, appropriate, I guess.

We all had to go up to the casket and look at him. My mother, at this point, was in a state, as my aunt called it, and wasn't up to making us do anything. It was my Aunt Bernice, my father's sister, who said we had to. "What will people think?" she said. "His own children slouched against the walls like a pack of ninnies! It's the last time you'll see him on this earth."

First Pat and then Jennie went up to this mammoth, polished piece of furniture. It had the lid up like an exaggerated music box, and I thought it would play a tune and the wax figure in it would do something, sit up, move its hand in time to the music like a band leader, something like that. But nothing happened. The figure, yellowish with rouged cheeks, lay there swamped by ruffled, snowy satin. It sort of resembled my father.

Aunt Bernice pushed me closer. "Say good-bye to your father, dear," she said, "and say a little prayer for his soul."

People were starting to line up to talk to my mother. The funeral director came in with a basket kind of thing, stuffed with flowers, and placed it on a stand near the casket. I looked at the dead guy in the casket and then at the funeral man who was propping a card up against the flowers. He was a plump, pink man with greying hair slicked back smoothly at the sides. He pulled at the roses in the basket with fussy, sausage fingers, displaying them better, making a show. That's when I must have pulled the revolver out of my pocket.

As a matter of fact, it *was* loaded. But I missed.

I've pretty well straightened out now, they think. It really was my father in the box and the funeral director was not responsible for his death, only for turning him into a wax dummy. But it's his job to do that, and not a criminal offence, and anyway, I shouldn't have tried to take the law into my own hands. I understand all that now.

My mother began to dwindle after that – dwindle and fade. My sisters took over the mother work. Pat already had her driver's license. She took things to the cleaners, brought home bags of groceries from the supermarket. She took me to the dentist. Jennie figured out how to cook. Mother wafted. She hardly ever went out, but slipped silently from room to gloom-filled room, glancing through a window, straightening a book.

On Saturdays Pat and Jennie sat around the kitchen table drinking coffee, doing the crossword in the paper and reminiscing.

"Remember that time we found Mother's wedding dress and we dressed up and you put on a suit of Dad's," Jennie said to Pat. I said (and I had to say it twice because not only do they not see me, they can't seem to hear me either) I thought it was me in Dad's suit, but they said I was too young at the time. They said I once put on my father's size eleven shoes and then wet my pants into them. I don't remember that.

Pat said, "Remember when Mother redecorated the living room and let us draw on the walls before the new paper went up?"

Jennie said, "Remember when Coco was hit by a car and he bit the driver when he got out to help him?"

"And he needed stitches," Pat said. "The driver, I mean."

"But Coco didn't die," I said.

"Pardon?" Jennie said. They looked at me funny and kind of frowned.

"Remember when I learned how to swim?" I said. But they didn't hear me, or else they didn't remember. When I was little I could swim all over the place under water, but I couldn't swim a stroke with my head sticking up. My father said I was still at the tadpole stage.

"Your mother's got so thin you could practically spit through her," Aunt Bernice said. It was true. She hardly took up any space at all. Aunt Bernice had been visiting on a daily basis. She moved in – just temporarily, she said – when Mother went to stay in the clinic. "A month or two will see your mother right."

Aunt Bernice is a stiff-upper-lip kind of person, a let's-look-on-the-bright-side type, which is usually pretty comforting, except when there is a sudden blow. She came back from talking to my father's lawyer one day looking weighted down. Everything that could sag did, eyelids, mouth, shoulders, even the hem of her skirt. She told us to leave her in peace for an hour until she could regroup her resources. We went into the kitchen leaving her in the living room contemplating her hands stretched out over her bony-looking knees. In the kitchen, Pat and Jennie kind of melted together and became this sort of fused single being with four sad, staring eyes. I don't know what I looked like. I sat on one of the high stools we had and kept thinking about whole walls falling over, wham! like the sides of a box, like flimsy pre-fab walls, wham! one by one, wham! Later, when Aunt Bernice was more like herself, she said to us, "Never, never allow yourselves to fall into debt."

Aunt Bernice told us we would have to sell the house and live with her, just temporarily. "It's way too big," she said. "Too much upkeep. Don't look so worried," she said to my sisters. "We'll all survive, one way or another. Chin up," she said to me.

Mother said she felt safe at the clinic. It's only half an hour away by bus and I went to visit her quite often. She put on a little weight. Most of the time she recognized me. I asked her about

Coco once, but she didn't remember him. I said, "Remember when I learned to swim?"

"Under water," my mother smiled. The pleats went out of her forehead and she looked happy. "Tomorrow," she said, "we'll take the boat and have a picnic at Sand Point." She was looking out the window when she said this, at the snow falling in fat, wet flakes. The benches on the clinic's scrappy front lawn looked soft with white cushions. You could lie on them and be swamped in cold satin forever.

Little by little, we started clearing our things out of the house, Aunt Bernice saving some of the important stuff, like my father's briefcase which she gave to me because I'm the boy, and Pat said, "How sexist can you get!" And a framed black and white photo of Mother looking off into the distance which she placed on a table in her tiny living room. Most of the furniture went into storage, except for the things that got sold. "Everything in the house that's nailed down stays," she said. She meant the mirrors in the bathrooms and the framed full-length mirror decorating the downstairs front hall.

Living at Aunt Bernice's isn't so bad. It's a small house which makes you feel snug, tucked in. Next door there's a family with nine kids. They sleep three to a bedroom. I was over there yesterday and I asked, "How do you sort everything out, like what belongs to you and what belongs to your brothers and sisters?" I wasn't even thinking about things like socks or hockey equipment or ballpoint pens. I think I meant, didn't their pasts get muddled up?

"We share everything," Tim said. He's my age.

"Everything?"

"Most things. If it fits, it's yours. If it doesn't fit, pass it along." Their mother was yelling at someone to turn down the TV, and one of the little kids was howling because he had his fat leg stuck between the uprights in the railing on the stairs, and one of Tim's sisters kept staring at me as if she liked me. A lot goes on in that house. I get the feeling it's a very solid house.

When I was leaving, Tim twitched his head in the direction of his sister who was running just then to answer the phone. "She likes you," he muttered. "She thinks you're good-looking or something." He kind of shifted his eyebrows up and down when he said this and I screwed up one side of my mouth and made a snorting sound. When I went back to Aunt Bernice's I looked in the mirror. I turned my head a bit to check out various angles. I hadn't felt this much like smiling for a long time.

The day we actually handed over the house to the new owners, Pat and Jennie cried. Aunt Bernice tried to comfort them, but Pat shrugged her off and said, "You don't understand." Jen ran outside and lay curled up on the back seat of Aunt Bernice's car so she wouldn't have to look at the house disappearing.

While Aunt Bernice collected the few cleaning items we'd been using, I walked into and out of each hollow room. Through one bleak window I saw the new owners, waiting in the driveway beside the moving van, waiting to carry in their boxes of things. Two little kids chased each other around our tulip bed as if it had been in their lives forever. The mother and father were looking up at the house, pleased, sure of themselves, sure of who they were, sure they had made the right move. They looked as though they knew that their lives were all squared away in their boxes and that soon they would be able to unpack and start living it up. I didn't mean to slam the door when we went out. It just banged shut like a gunshot. Loud enough to wake the dead. Aunt Bernice and Pat both jumped, and I saw Jen's face, wide-eyed, pop into sight framed by the rear window of the car.

A couple of years can make a big difference in a person's life. Mother is able to come for weekends and we don't feel awkward around her any more. We can discuss things. "I hear the house is up for sale again," Aunt Bernice told us. Just the three of us were sitting on the back porch catching a few rays of spring sun and guessing which day the tulips would open up. My sisters were off doing important things in their own world.

"They haven't been in it long," my mother said. Her voice was low but she looked all right. "It must have been only two years ago that we sold it?"

"Almost to the day. Do you remember that?" Aunt Bernice asked me. "Pat bawling and Jen hiding in the car and you wandering around like a zombie muttering under your breath. I finally had to take you by the arm and drag you out. Remember? What on earth were you going on about?"

"I remember," I said, but I didn't tell her what I was going on about. Now that I'm that much older, I would be embarrassed to tell her about the hex I put on the house. Well, a sort of hex. Actually, I made a wish. I said over and over, I wish they would never see themselves in the mirrors, but only see me and my sisters, and my father alive, and my mother packing a picnic lunch. For ever and ever.

TARGETS

Judith Freeman

Zak Walchuk jabbed the red button, one, two, three times. Blue lasers arced into space. One, two, three hits and the alien space station vaporized. Ecstatic, he zeroed in on a remaining alien fighter.

"Easy does it," he whispered as the fleeing craft wavered in and out of his gunsights. His thumb hovered and then, staccato-like, fired. The alien ship burst apart.

Sighing, Zak sat back and dropped his trigger on the blanket. After nine games in a row, his right thumb ached. So did his eyes.

He rolled to his feet, flicked off the screen, and stepped to the window. Venus and Mars had drifted behind the apple trees while he had decimated aliens, but a three-quarter moon lingered, outlining the sweet pea frame and tipping the gladioli with silver. Zak cranked the window open and savoured the scent-laden air. Sweet peas were Ma's favourite, he thought. She'd have enjoyed this summer's crop.

A black shape rose up from the strawberry bed. "God?" it asked, ghostly arms spread.

Zak flinched. His father Abe was out there, alone, mumbling. But even though Zak forced the air to stop whistling up his throat, forced his thudding heart to slow, the bits and pieces of words he netted out of the darkness made no more sense now than they had at the supper table. Cold, clammy dread returned.

"But, God, I can't . . ." Zak's father swung his moon-limned arms and whirled around so that Zak saw the anguished eyes, the rictus of silver teeth. "You ask too much." He groaned and covered his face.

Zak let out his breath and backed up until his legs hit the bed. Slowly, he sat and then, convulsively, scrambled under the covers and pulled them so high he could see only the moonlight coldly fingering his computer. Trembling, he stared at the blank screen, right thumb twitching.

Zak clung to the image of his mother, the way she looked before the cancer took her, all rosy and smiling, golden hair tossed by a late winter chinook. But he couldn't keep the smile on her face or the bloom in her cheeks, and he nearly cried when she faded and he had to open his eyes to his dawn-washed walls.

His oldest jeans and rattiest sweat-shirt lay near his head, and his father stood at the door, gesturing at him to get up. Zak stumbled to the bathroom and then into his clothes. His fishing clothes. He hadn't been out to the lake for weeks. Fish don't bite in the summer heat, his father had said.

There was no sign of breakfast, just an ashtray piled high with butts, so Zak grabbed his Abe Walchuk Haulage cap from the counter and pelted out to the garage. His father came out with an armload of kindling and jerked his head toward the driveway. Zak took the wood to the truck. He made two more trips before his father clanged the garage door shut and trudged down the drive with a gasoline can and a tackle box.

Two kilometers down the Trans-Canada, Zak remembered to ask about breakfast. His dad grunted and lifted a hand from the steering wheel. Zak interpreted the gesture to mean "later." He settled back. He could wait. He had waited for the fishing trip, hadn't he?

His eyes drifted across the fields, still weighted with their purple blanket of shadow. By the time they reached the Cypress Hills turnoff, the sun would be up and he might spot some of the antelope that lingered in the folds of the first rise of hills. Zak yawned. An antelope jumped and ran like a video hero racing across fantasy kingdoms to rescue the princess. Zak twitched his thumb. A dun brown figure leapt into flickering action . . .

This time, Zak heard a meadowlark's liquid prayer and smelled sage's dusty incense as he struggled to open his eyes quickly. He expected to see blue lake water. Instead the Walchuk truck was parked in the shade of a small stand of pine. Zak hopped out, puzzled, and joined his father on a grassy knoll.

They stood on the lip of the Cypress Hills, its ancient snout thrust into the prairie grassland below.

Abe Walchuk hawked and spat. "Is this the land of Moriah, Lord?"

Zak gulped at the cold thrust of fear in his innards. There was only his dad and him and their truck here. And the truck wasn't called Lord.

"Dad?" he quavered. "Dad, you all right?"

His dad had a worn look, like he'd been up all night. "Dad?"

Abe turned away. And after a moment, Zak followed him back to the truck. Abe stuffed an old gunny sack with the kindling and handed it to Zak. Then he picked up the tackle box and the gas can and set off.

"What about the food, you know, breakfast?" Zak puffed, struggling after his father into the trees.

"God will provide," Abe muttered.

Zak clamped down, hard, on the twisting fear. He forced himself to focus on the familiar red gas can. It bobbed in his father's hand, in and out among the trees and then down the side of a coulee thick with chokecherry bushes. He told himself he was stalking an evading alien target. He'd get it, sooner or later.

By the time he staggered up a sandy crest and dropped his sack beside the can, he had convinced himself that the pain gnawing at his gut was hunger from the chase.

He looked around. They were closer to the prairie floor but high enough to mark the green line of a creek snaking through the grasses.

Above them a hawk floated, head to the wind. It was an easy target, he thought, thumb cocked on an imaginary trigger. Too slow to be a sporting hit for space lasers, though. He thrust himself into the role of the hawk, looking down. Nothing moved in the sun-seared grasses.

"There's no lake here," Zak said, instantly back in his own head. He braced for a clip on the ear.

Instead, his father reached for the sack, dumped it and poured gas over the kindling. Then he took a knife and whetstone from the tackle box and began to rub them together.

Fascinated despite his unease, Zak edged closer. The rasp of metal on mineral seemed to match rhythms with the buzz of invisible cicadas. He sat, mindful of lurking cacti, and dropped his sweaty cap on the grass. His stomach growled. He wondered if there were sandwiches in the tackle box. Just beyond his cap, something furtive scrabbled in dry grass. Zak held his breath. A small animal perhaps. He thought of the keen-eyed hawk and looked up. It was gone. Zak relaxed.

Then, abruptly, his father stood.

"Now, Lord?"

Zak tensed. A single raven's croak floated between them.

"But . . . he's a child." Abe choked on the last word.

Zak froze. He couldn't jump, couldn't run. Suddenly his father wrapped his arms around him. Zak squealed but his father only gripped him tighter.

"All right, all right. I heard you the first time," his father muttered. Zak, struggling now with intense fear, knew his father wasn't talking to him.

"I don't know if I can do this, Lord."

Then Zak was dragged to his feet. His legs wouldn't hold him and he sagged against his father's iron embrace. He felt cold metal touch his cheek. He couldn't breathe. Lights, like multi-coloured lasers, pin-wheeled in explosions across his eyes. Then, unexpectedly, he was free and on the ground again. As he weakly rolled over, his father raised the clenched knife.

"Praise the lord!" Abe screamed and the arm descended, the fingers relaxed, the knife flew.

Thwunk!

When Zak, between one heart beat and the next, realized that the knife had not split him in two, he allowed his breath to seep slowly out and his head to loll feebly on the grass. The quivering handle of the knife came into view, then his cap, split across the brim, spreading with the red blood of a very dead rabbit.

"Hallelujah!" His father dropped to his knees and pulled Zak into his arms. "The Lord will provide," he exalted, "the Lord will provide."

HIGHER ANIMALS

Jay Henderson

Skye's heart fluttered like a bird in a cage – a wild bird, only moments trapped. They were out to get her, no doubt about that, and they always seemed to get what they wanted.

"Just about got you covered, Skye," wheezed Kevin, nearly out of breath from the chase.

"Hurry. Get yourself out of sight, too," Skye coaxed. She was amazed that Kevin had stuck with her, knowing how dangerous it had become. He was being uncommonly brave, offering to cover her first and then look after himself. She felt him toss a few last handfuls of poplar leaves over top of her. Then he made rustling noises burrowing into a separate pile they had prepared together. Skye inhaled the musky smell of decaying leaves, her nose pressed sideways against the cold and spongy forest floor. She prayed their tormentors would pass without detecting her red hair through the kaleidoscope of autumn colours. Otherwise she would end up dead and decaying too, if she weren't hidden well enough.

Neither said a word from then on. Everything was so quiet and still, Skye allowed herself the luxury of thinking that she and Kevin might have outsmarted their pursuers. Unfortunately, that possibility rapidly dissolved as the derisive howls of the Hasher twins once again rang through the chill air.

It was clear that the twins had come over the ridge and were bearing down upon the hiding spot. One of them came crashing through the bush nearby, sending shock waves into the earth. The side of Skye's face tingled as it picked up the vibrations. Was it Katie or Marla? Strange that one of them was running ahead of the other. The Hashers were weird; fourteen years old and still as inseparable as honey on toast.

Whoever had run ahead was getting closer. Closer and closer. "We're gonna eat you two scum-bags for breakfast!" she screamed. It had to be Katie, Skye thought, judging by the raspy voice.

"Pack rats!" added Marla, catching up. Her yelp was unmistakable.

"Come on, you freakin' squirrels, show your faces!" bellowed a third voice: a boy's.

Oh no, not that new guy! troubled Skye. Not fair; not fair at all. We're dead meat! We might have had a chance against the twins, but from what I've heard, this – what's his name – Todd, is an animal. They say he loves to see fear in his victims' eyes before he does them in.

Skye believed her heart would soon give her away. It was thump-thumping against her rib cage with the force of a tom-tom. One of them is bound to run right over us, she thought; there'll be a scream, and we'll be at their mercy. I know what they're like. I've seen Katie and Marla operate back at school. They never show sympathy for anybody smaller or weaker than themselves.

Rustling sounds. Someone was almost on top of her! Then a *craaack!* right next to Skye's head. The sound shot into her ear, but she remained frozen. She hoped Kevin was staying still, holding his breath also.

All fell silent. Her heart, starved for oxygen, slowed to the point where she was afraid it might stop beating altogether. The world seemed locked in a freeze-frame. Skye expected an arm to thrust through the leaves any second and grab her by the neck. But it wasn't a hand she felt.

Something warm was making its way up her pant leg, rubbing its hairy body against the inside of her calf. It scurried a few centimeters, stopped, scurried and stopped, scurried and stopped. Gross me out, it's a mouse! she panicked.

It reached her knee. God, how she wished she had worn tight-fitting pants; how she wanted to scream – jump up – shake her leg – tear off her baggy jeans – whatever it might take to get the stupid thing out of there! But Skye couldn't. No way! Her life was more important than some roguish rodent using her pantleg as a hiding hollow.

Skye was determined to remain frozen in place, no matter where the little intruder went next – almost – but she absolutely had to let the air out of her lungs. Pursing her lips, she let it out ever so slowly, until she began to grow faint. Then she drew it in again like sucking yogurt through a narrow straw. Nothing mattered but her breathing, certainly not a *harmless* mouse, she told herself with a shiver. But, she began to wonder, was her breathing controlled enough, or was Katie standing there glaring down at the mound of browns and yellows covering her, watching it rise and fall like a blacksmith's bellows? Surely the thin layer of leaves wouldn't be enough of a covering to save her from the three beasts of Redmond Junior High.

Then the mouse started inching its way up her thigh, heading for higher ground.

"Which way do you think the pond scum went, you guys?" Katie whispered. The others were close, too. Real close.

"I dunno. When they slipped over the ridge, I thought they were headed toward this big pine . . ." said Todd. "But now I'm not so sure."

"You hear that?" squealed Marla. "I bet they're escaping to the river, like all vermin when they're up against it." There were rustling sounds in the distance. The three immediately struck off.

Thwick! Katie's right foot clipped the heel of Skye's boot as she sped off.

Oh God, no! Skye thought, tensing from temple to heel. The muscles in her neck, back and legs ached like they were being pulled together by stretchable bands running through her body. Even the mouse, who had managed to scale her thigh, stopped stone still. Thankfully, the boots continued to pound the earth, and the vibrations were rapidly diminishing in force. She relaxed, imagining the ends of three taut elastic bands in her body slowly coming together at the centre.

Elastic. The mouse was almost up to her panty line – definitely going too far! But was it safe to jump up yet? Were they far enough away? It was obvious that Kevin hadn't mad a move yet. Reminding herself how serious the consequences of discovery would be, Skye decided to stay put a little longer. But the mouse had better not cross the elastic. If it moved, she moved!

Skye forced her mind, once again, to refocus. She thought it so unfair. The others had two obvious advantages: their superior strength and greater speed, compounded by the fact that they were ganging up. She knew it wouldn't matter to the twins that she wanted nothing from them, found it impossible to hate them. They were so much like their parents, competitive stock traders, both of them. They enjoyed the kill.

Then Skye remembered what had happened to her two friends, Tracy and Twig. They would never run away again. Katie and Marla got them good. Skye had stayed hidden, watching from a safe distance as the twins picked them off one after the other. There had been no choice but to hide – *no* choice but to hide.

Skye's mind reeled as the mouse darted across the elastic and shot halfway up her right cheek where it lay down, trembling like a low voltage, battery-operated massage unit. It tickled. Skye twitched her cheek. The mouse reacted quickly, making a break for it down the back of her leg and out the end of the pant tunnel, scratching her with its tiny claws all the way.

"Kevin. Kevin, let's move it!" Skye commanded. She leapt to her feet. Immediately hunching back down, she checked all around. "They're bound to backtrack and sniff us out if we stay put."

"Oh, this is great! They'll never find us here, not a chance. How'd you spot it?" Kevin asked, huddled against the wall of a small cave, high up on the riverbank.

"Caught a glimpse of it out the corner of my eye. Probably an old washout. Maybe a grizzly dug into it for a den." Skye sat close to the entrance, scanning what she could see of the riverbank.

"What!" blurted Kevin. "Grizzly?"

"Shhhhh! Keep it down." That waterfall up the way would cover some noises, but it was better to be safe. Even if he had shown some courage earlier, Kevin was still no Robin Hood. She was pleased to have his companionship, though.

"Sorry," he whispered. "But if some smelly old sack of a bear once used this as a home and comes back to claim it, we're gonna be nothing but lunch."

"Kevin, I think I hear something."

"Oh shit, it's the bear. It's hibernating time again and we're . . ."

"Shhh!" Skye scolded, whispering, "don't say another word."

They both sat absolutely still, once again holding their breaths. Sure enough, there were noises – and soon, voices.

"Look, there's fresh tracks here!" howled Todd.

"Yep, that's one of them all right," spoke Katie, sounding as always like someone had rubbed the inside of her voice-box with sandpaper.

"C'mon, c'mon, they gotta be hiding right around here somewhere," yelped Marla. "Let's find 'em and toast 'em!" Skye pictured Marla with a string of drool running out the corner of her crooked mouth. She would be hanging at Katie's shoulder, making them look more Siamese than identical.

"Not so fast," said Katie. "There are more tracks heading further upstream. See? They've gone up past the waterfall into the pines. I'd stake my life on it."

"I think you're right," replied Todd. "Let's go, you guys. We have to put those two away once and for all!" The sounds of their huffs and grunts quickly faded away.

Skye, letting the air out of her lungs and gasping for more, suddenly found herself wrapped up in Kevin's arms. He, too, was struggling to get his breathing back to normal, but obviously couldn't contain his joy at having dodged the grim reaper again. "Ha! What a bunch of idiots," he said, "they couldn't track an elephant across a field of chocolate pudding."

Then he laughed. Skye laughed, too. They laughed and hugged, and rocked and laughed and held each other tightly in the middle of the little cave, right where the grizzly had probably rested its massive head.

All of a sudden, a head appeared in the entranceway. "Ewwww, you two look pretty cozy." Reaching in, Katie grabbed Skye by the collar of her coat and plucked her out. Kevin stepped out peacefully, not looking anyone in the eye, his face flushed and turning redder by the second.

Katie faced Skye head on, staring her down. "Now then, I think you've got something I want!" Suddenly her right arm shot forward, toward Skye's middle. Twisting her fist around as she thrust it ahead, Katie opened it palm up and ordered, "Put it there."

Skye immediately reached for the metal loop attached to her belt. She only had one life tag left, and was certain that Katie knew it. Disconnecting the loop from her belt, she slid off the piece of leather with the word SQUIRREL stamped into it, and placed it in Katie's hand.

"You are officially dead meat!" squealed Marla. "I believe the graveyard is up that way." Drooling more than she normally did, Marla pointed toward the hill where the Animal Game had started over an hour ago.

"So sorry – aren't we girls?" said Todd, his eyes gleaming like those of a wolf ready for the kill. Yanking Kevin's last life tag from his belt, Todd took off in pursuit of two orange-shirted upper herbivores who were making a break for the pines. Katie and Marla struck off as well.

As Skye and Kevin trudged toward the Animal Graveyard to twiddle their thumbs until the end of the game, Kevin took hold of Skye's hand, saying, "Next time, let's ask to be carnivores or upper omnivores maybe. We could be the grizzlies."

"Higher animals, eh? Grizzlies could be all right, I guess," Skye mused, squeezing Kevin's hand tightly. A broad smile floated across her face before she added, "How's your bear hug, Kevin?"

A MAJOR MALFUNCTION

Mike Kilpatrick

Whew! Made it.

I finished the last question and put down my pen. Maybe even passed this one. Wouldn't *that* be nice? My fingers felt stiff from writing, and I clenched and opened my hand several times.

The room had that artificial hush to it, the hush of a class during a big test. I listened. Overhead – the low, eternal hum of the fluorescent lights. Behind me – a muted rustling sound as Andy shifted in his chair. Around me – breathing. Yeah, I could hear everybody breathing. Kind of comforting. Outside in the hall, a locker door slammed shut. Voices and laughter echoed, then disappeared.

"One minute," Mr. Kent warned, jolting me back to reality. He leaned back against the heating vent and scanned the room. Behind rimless glasses, his eyes looked as grey as the January sky.

"Oh, sirrrrr!" wailed Mary Sinclair.

I glanced at my paper and my answer to question three. I'd written: "'Out, out brief candle' is from the famous 'tomorrow and tomorrow and tomorrow' speech. This is when Macbeth learns that the queen, who got him into the whole mess, is dead. It's a metaphor expressing how short life is."

Why couldn't Shakespeare write in English? I thought.

"Make sure you sign your names on the upper right hand corner of each page," instructed Mr. Kent. He rubbed the back of his neck with his left hand.

The gesture reminded me of my grandfather, who used to do that when he got tired. Grandpa Pat had died of a heart attack just before Christmas, and I couldn't keep him out of my head. I pictured him now, sitting upstairs, looking out his bedroom window, listening to the radio. That's how I'll always picture him: eighty-five years old, a bantam rooster of a man, sitting waiting to die.

I sighed. Our family expected it of course, but his death really threw me. I missed him, you know.

Click, craaaaackle, the intercom sputtered to life.

"Your attention please!" said Mrs. Lacey, our principal, her tone unusually grim. "I have a rather sad announcement to make. The United States shuttle Challenger has blown up on takeoff. It appears that all seven astronauts, including teacher Christa McAuliffe, have been killed."

Our class was stunned. Everybody stopped writing, and we all looked at each other. Nobody seemed to know how to react. The quiet of exam-time deepened. Time seemed to elongate. Tilt, ding, whoops! Something shifted inside me. I felt suddenly off balance.

Honest to God, my first impulse was to laugh. No kidding, it almost slipped out. I couldn't help it. I mean, the news surprised me. It seemed impossible.

Andy, my best friend, *did* laugh, a snort, then an incredulous giggle cut short by an embarrassed cough.

"It's not funny," Brad Anderson said from the seat beside Andy. Fifteen, six feet tall, Brad played quarterback for the junior football team and he thought he was real tough.

A guy on my left, two aisles over, was almost crying. His knuckles dug into his eyes. His shoulders were bunched as if he didn't want to be seen. I mean, you don't cry at our school unless you want to be branded a wimp.

I turned around to say something to Andy. Brad was towering above him, his face twisted with rage. He drew back his fist and – whap! Andy's head snapped back. His eyes opened wide.

"Hey!" I said, frightened.

"Boys!" Mr. Kent called sharply.

"What're you laughin' at?" Brad snarled at Andy, his voice breaking.

Mr. Kent moved towards them. "Brad, sit down."

"I don't think it's funny something happened to the shuttle," Andy tried to explain. "That's not why I laughed."

"You better not laugh," Brad warned, retreating to his seat. "You shouldn't laugh."

"Off my back, doorknob!" Andy told him, holding his jaw.

"That's enough!" ordered Mr. Kent. He looked shaken up, as if he wasn't sure what to do. That scared me. Mr. Kent always seemed so sure of himself.

Andy spoke softly, addressing not only Brad but the rest of us as well. "I didn't think they could die, that's all. Not *them.*" Andy's eyes stayed glued to the top of his desk. He didn't seem afraid or anything. Angry maybe. Confused. Hurt that people misunderstood his laughter.

The bell rang and we all filed out of the classroom. The hall buzzed with the news. I felt awful. I'd been going to laugh too. The announcement felt like a bad joke. I mean, people like that don't die. They're not supposed to. Heroes don't die. Sylvester Stallone never dies in his movies. Neither does Arnold Schwartzenegger. The thought of those astronauts dying was absurd, something you'd laugh at because you knew it couldn't be happening.

Andy and I went down to the student lounge. The place was crowded, all of us watching the TV perched up on a wall unit. "There they are," Andy whispered.

On the screen, the flickering figures of the crew walked out across the tarmac. Her hair a tangle of curls, Christa McAuliffe stepped out of the line for a second and said something into the camera. Her face crinkled with laughter, and in that moment she reminded me of a kid, like some of the girls I know, all excited when they're about to begin a wild roller-coaster ride.

And then the countdown.

Lift-off.

The explosion.

And afterwards . . . on the ground, the faces of the onlookers: confusion, fear, knowledge. Up in the sky, the long, white vapour trail falling silently through the air like some disconnected umbilical cord.

The first time we watched, I somehow thought maybe it wouldn't happen, maybe they'd made a mistake. Maybe, maybe, maybe . . . but of course I was wrong. During the next few replays I kept hoping for a different ending.

"Beam me up, Scottie," Andy said, shaking his head in disbelief. "This ain't how it's s'posed to go. This never happens on *Star Trek.*"

"Yeah," I agreed. "Where's Captain Picard?"

"Where's Data?"

Something held us there in the lounge. We skipped all our afternoon classes to watch the coverage; a lot of students did.

About two o'clock a bunch of kids came in, some grade twelvers. Leather jackets with studs. Spiked hair. They crowded up to the front and stood watching for a few minutes.

"So, like, how long's this stuff gonna be on?" a girl with orange hair and army boots asked.

"All afternoon," Andy said.

"Oh Gawd!" She rolled her eyes. "I can't stand it. We're gonna miss our soaps."

Her boyfriend scowled. He pulled at the safety pin stuck through his left earlobe. "They can't do that. We always watch 'General Hospital'."

"C'mon, eh?" someone said. "Be quiet. We wanna see this."

"I bet you do," the punker hissed. "You're the kinda creep who slows up to slobber over a car accident."

"Ghouls!" the orange-haired girl yelled as her crowd pushed their way out of the room.

That night they showed the disaster on the TV the whole evening. I kept switching channels to find the coverage . . . don't know why I was so fascinated. After all, what'd I care about that teacher? I never met her. Hey, I don't even *like* teachers. Maybe I *am* a ghoul. Still, without my wanting it to, her death really bothered me.

There they were again, the crew walking, arms swinging, Christa McAuliffe stepping excitedly out to say something, the ice-covered, glistening sheen of the bottom of the rockets, the countdown, the lift-off, and then . . .

I must've watched twenty re-runs. What began to strike me as weird and particularly gruesome was the conversation between Mission Control and the pilot.

"Challenger, go at throttle up."

"Roger, go at throttle up."

Orange mushrooming fireball . . . what the . . ? Something obviously wrong. Vapour trail stopping mid-flight, then forking.

"We're at a minute fifteen seconds, velocity twenty-nine hundred feet per second."

Mission Control's voice didn't change. That's what was so awful. There was no horror in it, no surprise, no emotion. He did pause though, and there was a long hush. Then, still in that mechanical tone, still unchanged, the voice continued.

"Flight controllers are still looking very carefully at the situation. Obviously a major malfunction. We have no downlink."

I turned the television off around eleven. The picture collapsed inward and then the screen went blank. Time to hit the sack.

Upstairs, I got into bed and turned on the radio. A talk show had some experts discussing the cause of the tragedy: politicians and scientists connected to the project, an astronaut.

I listened for a while and finally turned the radio off. I got up and padded into the hall. Grandpa Pat's room was across from mine. I opened his door.

A lingering whiff of pipe tobacco – his brand, Sir Walter Raleigh – hit me. Still around, after all these weeks. Towards the end, I used to come here every night. I'd wake up scared he was going to die, and I'd come in to check on Grandpa.

I'd stand in the doorway. Asleep, he'd be snoring. The snore came up slowly and rolled around in his throat. Sometimes it stopped.

I'd wait for it to continue but it had stopped right in the middle. I'd think, *heart attack!* and sneak closer.

He'd start to snore again.

Alert now, I'd watch him closely. Grandpa Pat slept on his back, his mouth grotesquely open. The snore would roll around in his throat again . . . and stop.

Oh man, he's dead! I'd think. He's stopped breathing for real.

I'd reach out to touch him, and his breath would catch like an engine starting up, and the snore would burst out again, making me jump with surprise.

Then I'd be scared to leave. As long as I was watching him, Grandpa would be safe. That's what I pretended, what I half-believed. All I had to do was concentrate and Grandpa Pat wouldn't die.

Now, here in the darkness, I looked at the empty bed. I felt like crying. He wasn't a hero or anything. He never fought in any war. He never went up in any rocket. I think Grandpa Pat had only been on a plane twice in his whole life.

I closed the door and went back to bed. I lay thinking, videos of Grandpa running through my mind: There he was, giving me a hug. White, soft, dandelion-fluff hair. As a kid, I used to love running my fingers through it. There he was again. We used to watch TV together – the late movie on Saturday nights. I remember Grandpa snorting with disgust at ol' Duke Wayne. "T'warn't true!" he told me. "Ain't no heroes and no villains like that. Just people, just us humans."

I remember the wood scimitar he made me one Hallowe'en, and the colourful shield he built from an old garbage can lid.

I remember playing peewee hockey at six in the mornings and Grandpa Pat watching me from behind the boards, his breath a plume of white smoke in the freezing cold arena.

As I fell asleep, the last image I saw was that white, white vapour trail falling silently in the sky like some unattached umbilical cord.

ALL IS CALM

Ann Walsh

I don't know how it happened, but I was the only one who could do it, and it was turning out to be worse than I thought it would be. I mean, I love my Grandma; everyone loves their grandmother, right? But my Gran had become, well, strange isn't quite the word. Mom said it was Alzheimer's and she cried when she told me. It didn't mean much to me at the time, but believe me, as the year went by I learned more than I ever wanted to know about that disease.

It makes people forget. Not just ordinary forgetting – the square roots of numbers or your last boyfriend's phone number – but serious blanking out, like the names of your children, where you live, what you do in a bathroom, and whether your bra goes on before or after you put on your blouse. My Gran didn't do those things yet, but chances were she *would* as the disease took her farther and farther away from the person she once had been. She still had good days, times when she seemed so normal, so like her old self that it made it worse when she went off into whatever strange place the Alzheimer's was taking her mind. She had always been a bit 'odd' – actually "ditsy" was the word my father used – but she had been kind and funny and caring and clean. Now – well, sometimes she was really different, weird even, and I was on a bus with her at four o'clock on a Wednesday afternoon hoping that today would be one of her good days.

I was the only one who could do it, take Gran to the doctor's appointment. Mom was away at a conference, my brother had to get his braces adjusted, and Dad couldn't get off work in time. "Katie," Mom said before she left, "Katie, she *has* to go. It took us months to get this appointment, and this specialist is the one who can help us get Gran into a home – he has to classify her condition as serious so that we can get her into a place where she'll be looked after properly. I can't do it any more; I just can't. She's only lived with us a year, but I can't handle her anymore."

I thought Mom was going to cry again when she said that. She'd been doing a lot of crying lately, so I put my arm around her and hugged her and said all the right things about how I didn't mind at all, and sure, it was just a short bus trip, and no, Gran wouldn't embarrass me and we'd manage just fine.

Sure. We were managing. Barely.

It started when I got home from school. Mom had left a note, reminding Gran of the appointment, and Dad had phoned her at noon reminding her again – but she hadn't picked up the phone, and I heard his anxious voice when I checked the answering machine. At three-thirty, an hour before we had to be at the doctor's, Gran was sitting at the kitchen table in her nightgown writing Christmas cards. At least she *thought* she was writing them. She'd taken the box of cards out of the drawer where Mom had stored them until next November, and she'd written her own address on every envelope – no name, just the address. She was singing to herself when I got home, singing Christmas carols and stuffing blank cards into envelopes – in March!

It took a while, but I got her dressed and we got out of the house and down to the bus stop in record time. The bus came along right away, and everything was going to be okay, and I was sort of proud of myself – and then she started singing again. "Silent night, Holy night, All is calm . . ." Gran has a loud voice, loud and friendly and the kind of voice you wanted to hear singing happy birthday to you when you were nine, but on a crowded bus it didn't sound friendly but just plain strange.

People turned around to stare at us, and I said "Gran, it's not Christmas. Don't sing those songs now."

She looked at me, and the singing stopped. Her mouth stayed open for a while, sort of caught in the phrase "mother and child", and then her face crumpled and she began to cry.

Out loud. Cry as if I had kicked her, or told her her puppy had been run over. "Don't cry, Gran," I said quickly. "Listen, you can sing all you want to once we get home – really."

She clutched at my hand, and suddenly the tears were gone. "We'll go carol singing," she said. "All of us. I'll make hot chocolate and we'll all go out in the snow and sing."

"Sure, Gran," I said, trying to untangle my hands from hers. "Sure, when Christmas comes we'll all go carol singing."

She smiled at me, and I gave up trying to get my hand away from hers, and just held it and squeezed it. Gran always had a nice smile.

She looked at you when she smiled too, right in the eyes, and you always knew that smile was for you and not for anyone else.

"Where are we going?" she asked loudly. "Why are we going this way? We'll get lost."

"It's the way to the doctor's office, Gran." I spoke really softly, hoping she'd get the idea and lower her voice, too. Again heads were turning, as people craned their necks for a look at my . . . for a look at the crazy old lady who used to be my Grandma. I tried not to meet anyone's eyes. "Shhh, Gran. We won't get lost," I reassured her.

It didn't make any difference. "Stop the bus, stop it, right now! We're lost!" she yelled. She tried to stand up, but the bus lurched away from a stop and she sort of fell backwards into her seat.

"Sit down . . . everything's going to be all right," I said. And then, just like the sun coming out, she smiled at me and, as if everything was normal and fine, she said, "Isn't it a lovely day, Katherine? It's so nice to spend some time with you, dear. Shall we go and have tea cakes after our appointment? You always liked those sticky buns they make at the Tea Shoppe."

She had come back again. Just like that. One moment there was this crazy old lady sitting beside me, and the next moment my grandmother was back. I don't know why, but suddenly I wanted to cry too.

"Sure," I said. "We'll go for tea and goodies." We sat there, silently, for the rest of the trip.

Then it was our stop and we had to get off. "Come on, Gran," I told her. "We're here."

She turned to me, and her face changed again, and she grabbed onto the seat in front of her and said, "I'm not moving. You're just trying to trick me."

"Gran," I urged, hoping that she hadn't gone too far away into the craziness of the disease again, "Gran, come on. The bus is stopping." I took her arm and tried to gently pull her to her feet, but she just clutched the handrail tighter.

"Leave me alone," she said, her voice now louder than it had been when she was singing carols. "I don't know who you are. I don't go places with strangers."

"Come on, Gran. It's me, Katie . . . Katherine. We're going to see the doctor. This is where his office is. Come *on,* Gran." The bus had stopped now, and the other people who were getting off had already left. I stood up and tried to pull her to her feet.

"Leave me alone. Don't touch me. Help, help me someone!" I couldn't believe it. She was calling for help as if I were trying to kidnap her – me, her own granddaughter!

"Gran," I said. "Please come with me. You know who I am . . . you've just forgotten for a moment. Please, get off the bus."

"Everything all right back there?" called the driver, and I could see him turning around and halfway rising from his seat. "I've got a schedule to keep, miss. You'll have to get her off right now because I can't wait any longer."

"I'm never going anywhere with *you,"* Gran said to me. "I hate you. You're a nasty little girl, and I don't know why you want me to go with you." The doors of the bus closed, and the driver pulled slowly ahead and I stood there in the aisle and wondered what on earth I could do. One thing I knew I mustn't do, though, was get angry. It wasn't my Gran talking. It was the disease, the Alzheimer's. I must remember that; Mom had told us over and over that Gran didn't mean to be cruel or to say horrible things to us, but the disease took over her voice as it took over her mind, and she couldn't always control the words that she said.

It's the disease speaking, I told myself, only the disease, not my Gran. Fine. But the stupid disease wasn't going to let her get off the bus, and what could I do about it? I put my arm around her shoulder. "Gran, Gran . . . please, try to remember. It's me, Katie."

The bus began to slow again, approaching the next stop. I didn't hear him come up behind me, but suddenly he was there. "Hi," he said, and then stood beside me, smiling down at my grandmother. "I have to get off at this stop," he told her. "Can I help you? Would you like to come with me?"

Gran was silent for a moment, and I was, too. I knew this guy, Kevin; he was in several of my classes this semester. He was tall, blond and into sports, not a type I hang around with. He always seemed to be clowning around with a group of kids, mainly girls, and I had figured he wasn't worth the effort of getting to know – just a jock who hung around with airheads. "It's okay," I said stiffly. "We'll manage."

But Gran was smiling up at him and taking the arm he offered. "What a nice young man," she said. "Yes, please, do help me. I think I'm on the wrong bus."

Kevin helped her out of her seat, then down the stairwell, and out the doors of the bus. He held out his hand as she stepped down to the curb, and she took it and smiled at him, as gracious as the Queen Mother. "I think your doctor's office is one block back," he said. "Would you like me to walk with you and Katie?"

"Katie?" said Gran, and for a minute I thought she'd forgotten me again, but then she noticed me and the glazed look went from her eyes and she, my Gran, not the crazy old lady, was back again. "Why, Katie, come on. We don't want to be late for the doctor, and then we're going for tea. Perhaps your young man would like to join us?" She slung her handbag over her shoulder and straightened the scarf around the neck of her coat and strode off down the sidewalk, heading in the right direction, walking tall and proud and normally.

"Thanks, Kevin," I said. "I'm sorry . . ." And then the tears that I'd been fighting with for almost the whole bus trip won the fight and I began to bawl.

"I know," he said. "It's really hard. Go ahead and cry. I'll keep an eye on her." He gestured to my grandmother, who had stopped in front of a grocery store and was staring at a crate of oranges as if she had never seen that fruit before. Well, in the world she lived in these days, perhaps there weren't any oranges. Or any apples or bananas or granddaughters.

"I'm okay," I said, and blew my nose. "Thanks again for your help. You were really great with her. I don't know what I would have done if you hadn't helped get her off the bus."

Then it struck me. Here was this guy I barely knew, big-shot jock and classroom clown – what was he doing helping out with my ditsy grandmother?

It's almost as if Kevin read my thoughts. He grinned at me. "Yeah," he said. "Didn't you know that your grandma is my type?"

I grinned back. "No. But then, I guess I don't know you well enough to know what your type is, do I?"

"We'll work on that," he said. "I think we've a lot in common, more than you realize."

"A lot in common . . ?" I began, then I saw him looking down the street at my Gran and I remembered how patient and good he'd been with her, how he'd gotten her off the bus when I couldn't, and suddenly I understood.

"Your grandmother, too?" I asked. "Your grandmother has Alzheimer's?"

"My father," he said, and he began walking towards Gran. "The doctors say it's 'early onset,' which means it starts when someone's younger. He just turned forty-six."

"Oh," I said. "I'm sorry." And I was. Sorry for Kevin and what he had to go through as his father went away to that special hell where people with Alzheimer's live; sorry for my family and me for what we had to go through with Gran; sorry for the embarrassment and pain and ugliness that was ahead and couldn't be avoided.

I was sorry for us all, but I knew we'd get through it, we'd survive. But my Gran and Kevin's father, they wouldn't get through it. They *wouldn't* survive except as lonely shadows of themselves in a world where nothing made sense and no one was familiar.

I went up to my Gran, who was still staring at the oranges, and right there, in the middle of the sidewalk with people all around us and Kevin staring at me, I gave her a hug. "I love you, Gran," I said. "I'll always love you."

She looked me right in the eyes, and smiled. Then, from somewhere far, far away she said, "I love you too, Mary."

OLD MATT

Ann Goldring

My dog, Matt, hates the heat. I watch him cross the road, stop at a tree, wet it. Too hot to walk. He sniffs the damp earth, drops to the ground, a heap of thick fur, sad eyes, long tongue.

Bill skids by on his new bike, a bright red job, ten gears and fast. Dirt flies in Matt's face. He yelps.

"Show-off," I yell. I'm mad. "Watch the dog, ya bum." I grab my bike. No one bugs my dog. Matt's old. Too old to run, too old to fight.

I chase Bill down the street.

"Wait up, scum." I shout real loud. Bill, he just rides on.

There's an ice cream shop on Main Street sells thick shakes and three-scoop cones. I count my change. Great!

"Lime an' fudge, please." Bill knows I'm here. I see him cross the road, walk real slow, slide through the door.

"Want some?" I ask.

"Yeah."

"Leave my dog be," I say. "Leave Matt be. He's old."

"Who? Matt? Yeah," he says. Slow and mean is Bill. He saw the dog.

"Leave Matt be," I say. He pouts his lips. I want to smash his face.

Bill takes a bite. His mouth is huge, his grin too wide. I yank back the cone. A big scoop stays stuck to his puss, then slides. Down his chin, down his new shirt, his clean shorts, lands on his shoe.

Lime green slop and fudge.

THE BOY, THE BALLOON, AND OPEN BLUE

Heather Haas Barclay

When the boy came to the new country he brought only his knife. The knife had belonged to his grandfather for many years.

"We cannot carry much in our arms," the boy's mother said. "We will remember."

The boy's grandparents were too old to start again in the new country. They hugged the boy and said he needed to be free. When they were young, they told him, they had been free to go anywhere.

But the boy wanted to stay behind with his grandparents who had cared for him while his parents worked in the city.

"Perhaps," the boy's father said, "when we have made enough money to buy a fine house, your grandson will learn to fly an airplane and he will come back for you."

The boy nodded hard.

The grandparents rocked gently. They smiled and their cheeks squeezed round and red.

"Perhaps," they said, standing up at the same time.

"We have heard," the boy's grandmother said, "going to the new country takes a long time." She brought the boy's parents bread and cheeses for the journey. She gave the boy's mother seeds for her garden.

His grandfather closed the boy's fingers around the knife, the same knife he had used to whittle wooden birds for the boy.

When the boy's parents returned to their room in the city they gave the food away because they could not carry it with them. The boy's mother put seeds for sunflowers, cucumbers, squash and pumpkins in the hems of her skirts.

The boy thought the seeds had spoiled as the family slept in crowded rooms, sat on damp trains, and stood in long lines waiting for bread, blankets and official stamps on the papers they won by outwaiting others. Finally, the man from the new country spoke to his father and told him the boy's family had permission to leave.

From behind high wire fences the others watched the boy going. His mother and his father held his hands. They did not look back. In the open blue the boy felt as though the plane stayed still while the world unrolled like a sacred silver scroll.

When they arrived his mother carefully undid her hems to uncover the seeds. She pinched each one like a miser counting coins, then placed them on mismatched plates according to their variety.

"We will be at home here," she said to the seeds.

The boy spread his arms to measure the space of his own room, the space from his room to the bathroom, the space in the kitchen, the front porch, the backyard.

The seeds his mother planted grew. Sunflowers shielded the porch. Squash blossoms hung from cedars at the driveway and cucumbers like fingers clutched and pulled on the little carpet of grass in the backyard.

Warm summer evenings, the boy and his parents sat on their porch on a couch they had found beside a curb. Neighbours mowed their lawns, clipped their hedges, weeded and swept, talking louder than necessary, occasionally throwing their eyes at the strangers on the legless couch on the porch. The boy's mother would go inside and stir the large pot she had carried to the new country. The boy's father slept briefly before leaving again for his second job.

At times neighbour boys gathered in front of his house. With shouts and whoops they would return to the street, crisscrossing their bikes in quick arcs. Once, a boy came toward the porch to speak to him. He looked straight into the boy's eyes, as if the boy could understand. But he spoke full of roaring sounds like busy traffic. When the boy did not reply, he went back to his friends, jumped on the seat of another boy's bike to show how two could ride at once. But the boy was afraid to let anyone take him anywhere farther than where he was.

One morning the boy heard a distant sound, velvety shooshing in the open blue. He stood on his porch, searched the sky and saw a rainbow balloon floating toward him. As the balloon approached he could see two people, no bigger than his mother's sunflower seeds, standing inside a wicker basket attached to the beautiful balloon. The tiny black shapes waved to the boy. Running along under the balloon's path, the boy waved back. The boy ran until the river that wandered through the city stopped him.

After the balloon had shushed into a tiny speck, the boy stayed in a field full of lace and daisies and purple-tailed flowers. He sat for a long time at the river's edge. There he watched ducks skid in to swim and otters somersault; he heard crows curse.

Every day he returned to the field.

He sat by the river, sometimes whittling branches with his knife, remembering the owls, the bluebirds, the swallows his grandfather carved while the boy had lived with him. Here the boy discovered many secrets: Heron's, as he waited to beak-spear a fish struggling in the shallows; Dragonfly's, stitching her needle body through the air; Starling's, watching flat-footed ducks preen; Fish's secret, hurtling into shrinking sunlight on a quiet evening. And Sky's too, always changing, filling and folding with clouds, trailing streamers of planes, buttoning designs of stars, sweeping storms into swelling monsters that shrivelled like genies into polished blue bottles.

One day, the boy watched green light and grey rainsheets wrap the world outside his window. After the thunder shushed itself, rumbling only now and then like hunger, the boy walked through the wet streets to his river field. The sun seemed to shake itself awake and the grass and flowers sleepily stretched up again too.

By the river, under a willow tree, the boy found a long branch and beside it three young swallows still in a nest. The nestlings' mouths stayed open, their heads tilted back, and each time an adult swallow swooped by their bodies bounced. Reaching to a fork in the willow, the boy gently set the nest in place. Then away he walked, carrying the branch.

The boy thought the branch long enough to be a walking stick, but when he leaned on it, it bent. The boy noticed irregular little lines along the bark and as he was pretending they were magic runes the boy felt eyes behind him. He turned and recognized the adult swallow watching from her perch beside the nest. Then she flew from the branch to climb into the sky. Above the boy she soared, her body and wings pointed.

Like an arrowhead, the boy thought. He held his branch up, bending it carefully into a bow, and he imagined how he might shoot magic arrows through the open blue to land in the hard-packed dirt of his grandparents' yard.

The boy whittled an arrow, then one more every day and on each one he carved a secret he had learned since arriving in the new country.

Every day he aimed them way up into the sky across the river. As the boy carved more and more arrows, sometimes he did not want to shoot them away. But the boy wanted to spell his home more than he wanted to keep his carvings.

The sunflowers in the boy's garden began to bow their haloed heads.

"Soon you will not be so alone," his mother said, "you will go to school and learn about this new country."

The boy thought how he would be made to stay inside amid speech he did not understand and people he did not know. Instead of a beautiful arrow, the boy hacked a rough stick, pointed and full of splinters and shot it into the sky. He marched to the willow and pulled the empty nest out of the tree, stepped on it and pitched the pieces into the river. When the boy turned around he saw the swallow perched where the nest had been, cocking her head at him. For the first time since he arrived in the new country the boy wept.

Looking up into the sky the boy watched the swallow pierce higher and higher. Far away the boy could see the balloon that he had chased to the river. It floated toward him, its dragon breathing sound louder, the two specks in the basket bigger and the rainbow colours brighter. Too late, the boy thought, too late.

"Help," the boy heard faintly.

The balloon seemed to approach more quickly and the dragon breathing increased. The fire jet shooting into the rainbow colours panted. The boy could see that the two people were waving hurriedly at him.

"Help," they called out together. "Oh help us, help."

Then the balloon was coming down so quickly it seemed to be falling. The boy guessed that because of the willows and the balloon's quick descent the people needed help to find a landing spot. From his pocket the boy pulled the large handkerchief his mother made him carry and waved it at the people.

"Here, over here," the boy called, "you can land over here." The boy jumped up and down in the field.

The boy could see a piece of the rainbow had torn away from the balloon. As it made its way down, bouncing gently as it landed on the grass beside the boy, the swallow swooped by him.

"An arrow pierced our balloon," the woman said. Her blue-black hair, the way she almost scolded, reminded the boy of starlings at the river. She leaned over the wicker side to throw out an anchor. “You don’t know anyone who might have shot it?” she asked.

The boy hid the bow behind his back.

“We always caught them before,” the man said, holding up a bundle of arrows exactly like those the boy had shot into the sky, “but this one came so fast and its shaft was so rough, I could not stop it.”

They spoke in the boy’s language, their words leaping like deer, in the manner of the boy’s grandparents.

“And now,” the woman pulled on the lapels of her vest thick with embroidered dragonflies, “what can we do?”

The man stood very still watching as the silk of the rainbow balloon fell across the drying stalks of lace and milkweed.

All of a sudden the boy knew. “I will help you,” he said.

The man nodded. The smell of carnations and dried leaves in the soap his grandfather used and the wood shavings snagged on his pants and socks – these the boy smelled.

“I can bring a needle and strong thread, scissors and patching material.” His mother never threw away any of their worn clothes. The boy returned to the field with the things as quickly as he thought to fetch them.

The woman ripped the sleeve out of the lilac blouse the boy brought. She placed it over the seam and the man began to stitch around it. He sewed standing up, leaning forward from the waist holding the needle in one hand, a piece of the purple patch in the other.

As quickly as the boy wondered when the repair would be done it was finished. The man broke the thread with his teeth, smiling lopsidedly at the boy. While the young woman stretched the strength of the patch, the man climbed into the basket and stood patiently, looking down at the boy.

The boy nodded goodbye, backing up out of the way, his bow still behind him.

But the man interpreted the boy's nod another way, and after climbing into the wicker basket he held up his hands like a heron testing its wings for flight. The woman and the boy reached for his hands and the man pulled them into the balloon basket.

The dragon breathing machine blew hard into the collapsed rainbow silk. The boy watched it swell, feeling the anchor jolt the basket as the young woman placed it in the corner. From that same corner she bent to pick up the boy's last arrow, the one that had torn the balloon. She snapped it over her knee and threw the pieces out on the grass. The balloon began to rise.

To the boy the air had the quick coolness of early morning, and as the balloon rose the earth beneath seemed brittle. He wished he could throw the bow over the side, but the woman slipped it out of his hand very gently.

One by one she carefully shot his bundle of arrows toward the sun. With each shot the balloon rose higher and higher.

Even though the balloon took them high up the boy could see details of his house when he looked down. Sparrows perched on the sunflowers eating out the seeds. His mother stood in their kitchen putting cucumbers in glass jars. His father peeked under leaf flaps at pumpkins and ripening squash. The boys on the street biked by his house waving at his father, calling his name. His neighbourhood, the boy could see, was not so huge.

Higher still the boy saw the whole city. Tiny people pushed baby stollers, strode quickly along the sidewalks swinging briefcases, sauntered lazily looking in shop windows, and through it all the river ribboned like the drifting tail of a kite. This new city, the boy discovered, was not so huge.

Higher into the open blue they floated. His grandfather was there whittling with a new knife, his grandmother rolling out dough. They waved. The boy saw that they winked as they always did when they were proud. The boy saw the edges of the world sloping gently like the bank of the river by his field.

The woman had shot every one of the arrows the boy had carved. With their hands on the sides of the basket the man and woman gazed down as the balloon began to drift toward the earth. Below them the boy saw his arrows also changing direction, returning to the world.

One by one the arrows pierced the trees below and the leaves turned into gold, red, orange, yellow. The colours of tanned faces and outdoor work, of scrubbing hands and apples, of shined shoes and Sundays, of chatter, woodsmoke, of fresh pencils, of season's change. And the boy saw how he changed. He would walk to school, wave to the boys on bikes, even climb on a bike with one to ride double into the school yard. And at this school he would learn all about this new country. He would remember too. The world, after all, was not that huge.

WATER

Jean Rand MacEwen

"You know that your problems are all of your own making?"

The man behind the desk glared at the young woman. He was middle-aged, thinning hair carefully brushed over the advancing bald spot. He was neat, tidy, almost prim. The badge on his soiled shirt proclaimed his official status. The large metal sign hanging across the front of the desk read: Ministry of Visionation Guerdon and Persona Empowerment, Assistant Regional Deputy. The real status symbol was on the desk top – his name, Alden, in beautifully hand-lettered script on thick cream paper mounted in an antique frame.

The girl sat, eyes lowered, hands rigid in her lap, careful not to give offense.

"It's your own fault." His voice was flat, uninterested, final. The long silence was broken only by the faint purr of the languidly turning ceiling fan. Finally he said, "There is nothing I can do. You should know that." That should get rid of her, absolve him of any decision making. He checked his computer for her name.

"Kate – I don't know who sent you here." Too many people were sent asking favours. "There is absolutely nothing I can do."

Kate appeared not to be listening. It seemed that her whole attention was concentrated on the baby in the carrier, but her head bowed in acquiescence. Her thin shoulders slumped. Aware of her desperation, he turned back to the computer to study the display.

"How could you be so careless!" For the first time he let his eyes wander to the child. Its fate was no concern of his.

"With all your degrees in genetics and your experience in animal husbandry you can hardly plead ignorance." His finger stabbed towards Kate. "Why didn't you have an abortion? It was your duty."

"I couldn't," Kate mumbled. "We were isolated. I couldn't get transport. I couldn't leave the cows." The man called up another display on his computer.

"Oh yes. Three cows, two with calf, on fresh grazing. Very responsible job. How did you blow that?" His tone was merciless.

"One cow miscarried and died." Kate was neither excusing or justifying. "The other produced a congenitally deformed calf. It did not live. The cow later died of mercury poisoning."

"So instead of five healthy animals," the official droned on, "you ended up with just one. No wonder there are so many demerits on your record."

"I tried. I really tried. I did everything possible but you just can't combat. . . ." Kate's voice trailed away. Eyes lowered, she stroked the child's cheek.

"I see you have been demoted to a poultry farm near Uxbridge. Too bad you didn't miscarry along with your cows." Glancing at the thermometer, the official mopped his forehead and neck with a greyish handkerchief. Thirty-three Celsius. The air conditioner wouldn't kick in until the temperature reached 35C. He sighed. Why me? he thought. Why do I get all the problems? He jerked himself up when he realized that he was watching the girl twist a curl of the baby's hair around her finger. Only by avoiding such nonsense had he reached his present position. Rules are rules – or should be.

"You understand the ecosystem as well as I do." His voice was harsh. "There can be no excess population. Why didn't you get a birth permit?"

"We . . . Ewan and I . . . we tried." She didn't enlarge or make excuses. The official turned again to the computer flashing up a number of names, dates and medical notations.

"Don't see any problems here." As the print rolled up he seemed to pounce.

"Got it! Consanguinity and cancer! No surprise you didn't get a birth permit. Surely you realize that only through careful genetic scrutiny and control have we been able to eradicate cancer. Some old folks can remember the scourge it was. Such a painful way to die." He was aware of sounding rather like a grade school textbook and fell silent. He looked directly at the young woman for the first time.

In the space of a breath he saw not Kate but Carla, his Carla with her long brown braid and luminous grey-green eyes.

"You were careless and irresponsible," he said to Kate. Carla had been serious about her career, her promotion to Lavruska. He slammed the door of memory and regarded Kate.

She was tall, painfully thin, with fine red-gold hair. Her eyelashes and eyebrows were almost white. Being something of a social history buff, he knew that at one time such colouring had been considered attractive. He could even understand it. Too bad the child had the same colouring – but of course it didn't matter. It was a non-person.

Holding the infant's tiny hand, the young mother sat wordlessly beseeching his help. Damn this girl! And her illegal baby. He turned to the computer. Very softly Kate hummed an old lullaby as she rocked the carrier. Carla used to . . . Alden sighed and tried to ease the tension at his temples with probing fingertips. Damn again. He had not felt like this for years.

In his job the only way to survive was to be efficient, ruthless when necessary, and not go soft and sentimental. It must be the heat.

"How old are you?"

"Twenty-six next month."

Twenty-six years. Suddenly it all rushed over him. Could it be twenty-six years! Emotions rigidly suppressed, denied, forgotten for a quarter of a century threatened to overwhelm him. He felt again the small hot body in his arms as he paced the floor. Infantile gastroenteritis. His son, his beautiful little son, was burning up with fever.

There was no hospital, no life-saving saline drip. The child was too young to be considered a contributing member of society.

He took refuge in bluster.

"Well, what do you expect me to do? I can't give it a water ration. Here's the only sensible solution. Let me make out a euthanasia form for it. Sign now, and you don't even have to take it to the Thanatos Centre. I'll do it for you. Any usable organs will earn you extra merit points. With the state of your records at the moment you need any points you can get."

She regarded him with a look he did not at first comprehend. Pity? By what right does this helpless creature pity me! Kate firmly closed the protective cover over the child, zipped up her own outer garment and prepared to leave.

"Sit down. Sit down. Don't be hasty. Let me go through the records again. Maybe I can find . . ." The baby started to whimper. "What's the matter with it?"

"Nothing." She spoke with a vehemence he had not heard previously. Her pale, drawn face seemed to come alive. "There is nothing the matter with her. She is perfect in every way." The baby cried, its little clenched fists beating the air. He had forgotten how loud a baby's cry could be even through the outdoor shield.

"Oh, sit down, sit down. Thanatos is still your best solution. Best for both of you. It's quick. It's painless. End of problem." The firm voice. The official line. Ignore the tightening in his chest.

"You are still young. Find yourself another mate. Have a legal baby. You are not likely to run into consanguinity problems again."

She remained standing and slowly shook her head. Alden slapped his forehead with the flat of his hand and groaned.

"Oh no! Don't tell me you are one of those 'one life, one mate' freaks. How did you get into this mess?" Without waiting for an answer he jabbed at the computer keys again. "Well, I see your mate has been assigned to the water project at Moose Factory. You may be sure he'll soon have a new partner away up there."

"No, he won't." Kate repeated. "One life, one mate. That's us."

The baby was really screaming now, so she sat down and got a padded box with a safety catch out of her bag. Opening it carefully, she withdrew a small vial and put a few drops of water on a clean rag which she brought to the baby's mouth. The child sucked eagerly on it.

"There is a tiny bit of valium in the water. I hate to do it but it quiets her."

With the child quiet again, he repeated his question.

"How did you get into this mess?"

Leaning forward, Kate tried to explain.

"Don't you see? It wasn't a mess. It was perfect."

"What's its name?"

"Not it – her. Her name is Eweena Palabrowska."

"Palabrowska. A patronymic. Really quaint – haven't heard one used in years."

"Yes, it's old-fashioned, but her father particularly wanted her to carry his name." Kate paused. What could she say that would move this man? Probably nothing.

"We've been together five good years, and there were no problems until we applied for a birth permit. That's when we discovered that our great-great-grandmothers were sisters."

The official shrugged and studied his computer.

"Euthanasia is the only way out of your dilemma." As they waited while the computer ticked and grumbled Alden urged her gently, "I know it's difficult – termination. It . . ." He glanced at the child. "She can't live . . . you can't pull it off. It's the kindest thing you can do."

As information grudgingly appeared on the screen he went on. "I see you still have title to property in the city."

"Oh, sure." Kate laughed bittlerly. "A lot of good that will do us. I was down there once. You can still see where the houses stood near the water. They say the lake shore was a good five kilometers farther south at one time."

"Yes, that's right. I was out in a boat years ago and you can look down in the water and see . . ."

"That was a risky thing to do," Kate interrupted.

"You're right. But I was young and foolish." But, his common sense told him, not as foolish as you are right now, getting yourself involved with this girl's problems. To keep to impersonal matters he continued.

"I've seen what's under the water – all rubble and the remains of towers – but I really don't believe the stories of tall trees and wild animals, even small ones. Rats, maybe, but furry animals wearing masks?" They laughed together. Alden turned back to the computer, punching the keys irascibly. No point in risking his reputation, his position.

"I see your family had property up the Ottawa River – high enough to miss the flood.

There is a change of number for the owner. How come?"

She wished he had not dug up that old business but she answered.

"Over use of well water on the property. Trouble with the Water Authority. My cousins own the land now."

The man was not sympathetic.

"None of our ancestors had much sense about the preservation of resources, but you seem to have a family history of mismanagement."

Kate's back stiffened but she said nothing.

"Go on. How did they lose the property?"

"Insects."

"What about them?"

"I can't change the past. You know as well as I do." Kate sounded resentful and, strangely, Alden looked at her with some respect.

"Yeah, sure. The Insect Era. Pesticides killed both insects and birds, but only the insects came back the next year."

There was a whimper from the baby. Kate lifted Eweena out of the carry-case and held her against her shoulder while she patted the baby's back. The soft, milky smell of babies seemed to permeate the utilitarian office.

There was a loud burp.

"That's better." Kate looked foolishly pleased. "That's my good girl." She turned Eweena on her lap so she faced the man. The fading light from the dingy window caught the little halo of red-gold hair. The baby smiled. Alden tried not to look at her.

"Get to the point. What's this property to you now?"

"My cousins live there. I know they'll help me." Kate leaned forward eagerly. "There's lots of room in the old cedar house and my ration tickets will cover . . ." He cut across her rapid flow of words.

"They won't cover water."

She seemed not to hear the mention of water.

"If I could be assigned to that poultry farm up the road I know I could manage. Please? I can share my water allowance."

"Don't be ridiculous. Water for one person won't support two." He looked at her sharply, noting her skin, her clothes. "You seem to have had access to water already. Where did you get it?" he demanded.

Kate was unruffled. "When we were with the cows, there was a stream. Even though it looked marvellous it was heavily polluted with mercury. No one minded us using it for washing. It felt so lovely." Kate hugged herself remembering. "But of course I didn't let that water get near Eweena."

Alden shrugged. If he could have nailed her for illegal use of water he could have passed her on to a higher authority – but no luck. His eyes were on the baby but his mind was on his position. He did his job well. He was secure. There was no reason to let this girl and her illegal baby upset him now. The past was past. Over and done. But he hesitated.

"Well, Kate," he said slowly, "I can issue ration tickets for her, register her for social insurance, health insurance, unemployment insurance. I can give you admit cards for schooling and add her to your travel permits. But I have no authority over water."

Silence hung between them and the old computer whirred and clicked as it printed various official papers. Kate's personal file appeared on the screen right up to her posting to the Uxbridge poultry farm. Rapidly he removed the Uxbridge address and substituted another.

"Oh," Kate gasped, "That's the one near . . ." He silenced her with a glare.

"Computers can make mistakes. One poultry farm is like another."

Kate watched in silence as the updated information appeared on the screen. Alden could almost feel the warmth of the small hug the mother gave her child when she saw the change in her water ration. One digit had changed. Ten percent. That gave her 10 percent more pure water! The official glared at her again.

"I keep telling you there is nothing I can do."

"Ten percent more water" kept singing in Kate's brain, but she said nothing.

"Since you won't take my advice on euthanasia you'll just have to take your chances – and they are pretty slim."

"Yes, thank you." her eyes were shining. "Thank you. For the advice," she added hastily. Closing the ultra-violet shield over the child, she zipped up her own protection and left.

The official groaned, holding his head in his hands. The air conditioner started to hum gently. A distant whistle blew. The end of another day. But still he sat there, head bowed on his hands.

THE PATTERN OF MAGIC

Jennifer Taylor

The sight of wizards on the streets of Oona was so commonplace, no one paid any attention to a mere student sorceress as she wandered the market square. There was nothing specific Kara wanted, just to be outside after the long, dark winter.

Classes were cancelled for Equinox week, and most of the other students had gone home for the holidays. Kara wished she could return to West Harbour, but her parents had sailed south to the Rim Isles seeking spices for their bakery.

Kara passed a stall selling fresh cinnamon buns and the smell reminded her of home. She dug into her pocket and pulled out a half-penny.

The plump saleswoman smiled and handed her a still-warm bun.

The rest of the market square seemed empty. Most vendors had moved outside the city walls for the spring fair that opened at week's end. Kara had saved several pennies to spend amongst all the booths and bustle of the fair. Today she was happy to be walking out in the sunshine.

Kara pushed back her hood and felt the sun warm her face. Her dark hair danced with a breeze scented with the smell of cloves and leather and freshly dug earth.

She sighed as she saw the school's cook haggling over the last of the season's limp carrots and withered apples. Perhaps with enough stewing or steaming they could be revived, but Kara longed for fresh greens like fiddleheads or leeks. Already the kitchen's garden was showing signs of growth so there wasn't too long to wait.

When she had first arrived at the college, three years ago, she had asked her instructor why they couldn't just pattern food from seeds. Kara had only been twelve at the time, and could only do simple magic. Now, after all her study, she knew, although there were simple patterns, there was no such thing as simple magic.

And patterned food, even though it looked delicious, did not nourish as well as natural food.

As Kara licked the last of the sweet, sticky bun from her fingers, she noticed an old woman across the square. Seated by the doorway of the Spotted Hen, the woman looked up and beckoned. Curious, Kara nodded and moved towards the inn when a voice stopped her.

"I see you couldn't face going home for the holidays. No surprise after your disaster with the pigeons."

Kara whirled around to face a tall white-haired girl.

Loren smiled. "I heard about your plan to clear the pigeons off Old Sally's roof. I guess when the Mayor's prize peacocks got stuck and started screaming you must have realized your mistake."

Kara felt her cheeks burn bright red, whether in anger or embarrassment she wasn't sure. Trust Loren to find out about last summer. It had seemed like a good idea at the time. She had changed the pattern of the roof's surface so when pigeons landed they would stick; then Old Sally's cook could gather them up for his pies. It had worked the first night, but by the second the entire roof was covered by squawking birds of all kinds including the peacocks, and a small fox that had climbed up for an easy meal.

Loren had grown up in West Harbour with Kara but had come into her power early. She had changed her hair and eye colour so often, Kara couldn't remember what the natural colour was. Presently Loren had chosen white hair and purple eyes. She made Kara feel dull and ordinary with her natural brown hair and eyes.

Kara didn't want to even answer Loren's smug smile. She turned away, and the old woman beckoned again. Kara hurried toward the stranger like she was a long-lost friend.

"Trinkets and treasures, child. Perhaps I have something you seek." The old woman motioned to her wares displayed on a red cloth beside her.

Kara knelt to inspect the assortment of objects before her: small clay pots, beeswax candles, polished wood balls, even a mummified lizard. On the edge of the cloth were piled a number of bulbs. Kara reached out for a small bulb already showing green.

"How much is the amaryllis bulb?"

"Two half-pennies."

Kara opened her mouth to speak but was interrupted.

"Two half-pennies are a whole, old woman. Why not one penny?" Loren's voice carried over Kara's head. She had followed her over.

"I leave room to bargain, Mistress. Have you looked in the wooden box in front of you?" The woman ignored Loren and spoke directly to Kara.

Glancing down, Kara discovered a small box with no lid filled to overflowing. Bits of bone, feathers, sea shells, polished glass, strips of leather and ribbons, all threatened to spill over the dark wood sides. Hesitating a moment, Kara reached inside. Her fingers closed around a small object.

She was filled with a sense of wonder as a tingle of warmth tickled her palm. Kara slowly uncurled her fingers to look. In her hand lay a tiny, pink, triangular tooth. She held it up to show the woman, who smiled.

"Two half-pennies, child. For both the tooth and the bulb."

Kara knew a bargain when she heard one, and quickly fished out her penny. As she moved to pay the woman, Loren almost pushed her aside to search the box.

Just as quickly her hand closed over an object. Her fist tightened as Kara tried to see what she had found. Loren's voice was unsteady as she asked, "How much?"

The woman shrugged and Loren was forced to open her hand. Kara could see a grey tooth much larger than the one she had just bought.

The old woman smiled. "Do you know what it is?"

Loren paused and her purple eyes narrowed. "It's a tooth. I can't imagine what I'll do with it. How much is it?"

The old woman focused eyes cloudy with age on Loren and smiled again. "A king's coin."

Kara gasped in surprise. It was an outrageous price. Loren seemed to pale almost as white as her artificial hair. Kara couldn't believe her eyes when Loren handed the woman a gold coin.

"For the tooth and a purple ribbon for my hair."

The old woman took the coin and nodded. "Good bargain, Mistress, and good day."

Kara would have been happy to never speak to Loren again but her curiosity was too strong. "Loren! How could you pay a king's coin for a little tooth? Mine was only a half-penny."

"Yours can't be very special then, can it?"

"Is yours?"

"Would I be so foolish to pay so much if it wasn't? That old woman was the fool to sell it so cheaply. She can't have recognized its pattern." Loren gazed from her clenched fist to Kara. Slowly she uncurled her fingers. "Do you know what this is?"

Kara looked at the grey tooth and shook her head. She wasn't sure she wanted to know what kind of creature had such deadly sharp teeth.

"It's a dragon's tooth," Loren said smugly. "And it is mine. I shall learn its pattern and create my very own dragon."

Kara shuddered. "Is that wise?"

"Wisdom has nothing to do with it. It is a matter of skill, something you don't have." Loren turned her purple gaze from Kara back to the tooth in her hand.

Kara had to protest. "It will take years to figure out the pattern with only a tooth to study." She fell silent at Loren's contemptuous glance.

"I can make my dragon in weeks, in less time than you can grow that flower." Loren pointed to the bulb in Kara's hand. "You don't even need to use magic, just add water. You've even got a headstart, there's already a bit of green showing."

Kara's hand tightened in her pocket and she felt the tiny tooth she had bought. She didn't recognize the pattern but the warm pulse of the shape made her bold. "I can do better, Loren. I can grow the bulb and pattern where this came from." She held up the small pink tooth.

Loren laughed. "How can you create something if you don't even know what kind of creature it will be? This is almost too easy. Shall we make it a formal challenge? So all the school can see you fail."

Kara paused to take a deep breath before answering. A formal challenge meant Master Eltarc, head of the college, would judge the results. Kara shivered at the thought of losing in front of everyone, but she nodded her acceptance.

Loren's delight was obvious as she skipped away. She turned once to call back to Kara. "When I win, the whole school will know what I already know: you're not fit to be a sorceress."

Kara slowly walked back to the college. The sun was still shining but she didn't feel its warmth. How could she have been so stupid as to let Loren challenge her? She had just made Kara so mad she had to do something.

Kara fingered the tiny tooth in her pocket and felt her heart lighten as a picture began to form in her mind. She knew she could work magic – she had been studying nothing else for so long. This would be like a final exam. "And I better pass," she muttered to herself as she hurried through the stone archway to the school.

Two store-rooms, deep in the cellar of the college, were cleared for the challenge. Side by side, Kara and Loren worked, a thick stone wall separating them. Still Kara could hear Loren's ragged chanting through the rock as they struggled to capture the pattern of the beasts.

The amaryllis grew as the weeks passed, and Kara worked late into the night hours. She slept periodically on a bed of straw and ate when she remembered food had been brought. She studied the tooth even in her dreams, softly chanting its pattern, searching for elusive bits to the whole. Next door, Loren's chanting seemed endless, broken only by her shouts of frustration.

The morning the amaryllis burst into bloom with fiery red blossoms, Kara awoke from a refreshing sleep. Today was the final day of the challenge: to recreate the pattern of the tooth for Master Eltarc and the school. Kara combed her hair and slipped on a fresh tunic over her shift. She held the tooth one last time, although by now she knew every bit of it.

At the knock on the door, she laid the tooth in the centre of the room and went out into the main hall. Loren was already waiting, her face as pale as her white hair, her eyes more red than purple as the strain of the past few weeks showed. Kara was tired but she would not give Loren the satisfaction of showing her fatigue.

The doors to both rooms were closed and locked. Master Eltarc stood between both girls, looking old and powerful in his formal blue robe. He raised his hand and nodded.

"Let the challenge begin."

Kara felt her stomach knot as the fear of failure gripped her. She swallowed hard as Loren began to chant her spell of creating. Kara wanted to run back into the locked room, or home to West Harbour, anywhere but here where she might fail.

She thought of the tiny tooth she had spent so many weeks exploring. She felt so connected to the tooth, it was as if it was calling to her to sing its pattern. Kara thought on the pattern in her mind. She opened her mouth and faltered as she sang the first note.

Already Loren had woven many layers of her own pattern with her strong soprano voice. Kara concentrated on the tooth and reached out for its warm pulse. The tingle of its true pattern seemed to envelop her, to give her strength, and she began to sing.

The entire school was assembled by day's end. Kara's throat was sore and her legs tired from standing but the song was complete. Loren sat slumped in a chair having finished a few moments before. Master Eltarc lifted his hand and the whole college grew quiet.

Kara held her breath as he approached her door. She could sense the creature's pattern enough to sing, but there was no telling what it might actually look like. As Eltarc turned the doorhandle he motioned for Kara to join him. Too nervous to sit, she jumped forward.

The heavy oak door swung open and Kara squealed with delight. A small dragon no bigger than a housecat sat waiting for her. A shimmering coat of green scales rippled in the torchlight as the dragon moved. He turned to peer at Kara, his jewel-like eyes twirling in happiness. He opened his mouth in a huge yawn to reveal rows of tiny pink teeth, and promptly fell asleep.

Master Eltarc turned to the second door. Kara watched Loren stand and smooth her long dress. If she was nervous, it didn't show. She saw Kara and smiled confidently. As Master Eltarc opened the door Loren moved forward. Her scream filled the hall and echoed through the empty upper floors of the college.

Loren didn't wait to hear master Eltarc's judgement. She brushed past Kara saying, "I am going to my room to sleep." Kara turned to Master Eltarc, who swung wide the door. There, lying on the floor, its huge mouth gaping open, rows of grey teeth snapping angrily, lay a giant creature.

"What is it?" Kara had to finally ask.

Master Eltarc winked at her. "A creature of the deep. We will have shark steaks with our fresh greens and fiddleheads for many weeks to come."

Kara ran back to her work room and laid a hand gently on her dragon's head. He made a soft sound like a purr as Kara began to laugh.

WAS IT FUN ON THE BEACH TODAY?

Budge Wilson

She had come down to the beach earlier than usual that morning. The air was clear, the shapes sharp and vivid against a cloudless sky, the sun's light still low and golden. An offshore wind blew steadily across the sand and out toward the dancing reefs. Standing up, facing the water, she could feel the cool air whipping her hair forward, as the breeze reached her from above the dunes. Shivering, she dumped her beach gear in an untidy heap on the ground and lay down beside it on the bare sand. Digging with her fists, she made two shallow depressions for her breasts, and wiggled into them. *There. It's warm down here. The wind can't get at me. Nothing can get at me. Not even Mother.* She pulled her swim suit – emerald green, tight – over her hips, and brushed her brown hair away from her face. Cat-like, she writhed on the sand and pressed herself into its warmth. *I'll have sand in my suit, sand in my hair. She'll say, don't track all that sand in over my clean floors. She won't even stop instructing me long enough to ask if it was fun on the beach today.*

"Hi, Julie." Mr. Desmond, the local beachcomber. Retired and bald, with skin like crinkle cotton. Bored and boring.

Julie sat up and hugged her knees.

"Hi, Mr. Desmond. Nice day."

"How come you're down so early? Your gang doesn't usually start cluttering up the beach till about 10:30."

"Cluttering?"

"Oh, you know. Frisbees and what you choose to call music. Splashing and shrieking."

You've forgotten how to be young, Mr. Desmond darling. She wished she could say it out loud. What satisfaction, what rich revenge.

"We're happy," she said.

He sighed. "Well, enjoy it while you can."

"Thank you," she said tartly. "We will."

He turned to go. "Your bathing dress is very pretty." It was clear from the turn of his head –

away from her – that he felt uneasy about his compliment.

Bathing dress. Out of the Dark Ages. She untangled her pile of beach paraphernalia and arranged them on the sand. King-sized bath towel with a two-foot-long Garfield, winking at her. She grinned, and ran her hand over his terry fur. Can of Coke. Sunscreen lotion from her mother, for protection. Baby oil, for a seductive shine. She moved her watch strap and admired the white ridge, one half-inch wide, declaring the depth of her tan. A book of short stories, summer reading for next year's Grade 11 English class, unopened. A *People* magazine, wrinkled and worn. A pair of mirror sunglasses. *If I'm a spy in the next war, I'll wear sunglasses exactly like these. When they interrogate me* (in her head, she said this word carefully, drawing out the four syllables) *I will stare at them with my two blank eyes, and they will be unnerved by my inscrutability.* She pronounced this last word slowly, too – this time aloud:

"In-scru-ta-bi-li-ty."

"Talking to yourself. Aha!"

She jerked around, startled. "Alicia! You could knock or something, to give someone a warning. You scared me right out of my skin."

"Why ya down so early?"

Julie stared up at Alicia through her sunglasses. *None of your business.*

"Because."

"Because why?"

Alicia thumped her heavy body down on the sand. Double chins. Five pimples. Julie counted them. Stomach.

"Because I wanted to be alone." *Did you hear that, Alicia?*

"Me too. Thank heavens for the refuge of sand and ocean for the comfort of the ravaged soul."

Julie looked at Alicia sideways. Not enough to have a bizarre name and a fat form. At fourteen, it's unappetizing to go around talking about ravaged souls.

"What in particular," asked Julie, spreading baby oil gently, languidly, over her smooth brown legs, "is ravaging your soul this morning?"

"Mother. She can't stop nagging. Or apparently she can't."

"You happen to be defining motherhood," said Julie, putting the top back on the bottle and arranging her towel on the sand. "About what?"

"Three guesses. *Fat.* 'Go easy on the cookies, dear.' 'Why not try jogging, this summer?' 'You'd *feel* better, darling, if you lost weight.' 'Out of the ice cream, Alicia.' 'When I was your age, sweetheart, I weighed one hundred and four.' Can you imagine such torture?"

"Yes."

"Huh. I bet your mum never nags *you.*"

"Don't be dumb, Alicia. If mothers didn't have anything to nag their kids about, they'd invent stuff." Pause. "Fathers are better."

"Sometimes," mumbled Alicia, bleakly.

The girls lay on their stomachs side by side. Julie glanced at Alicia.

"Him, too?"

"Worse." Alicia sighed. "Wants me to *help* all the time. Says I'm *irresponsible. Lazy,* even. Also loves to elaborate on the theme of Fat – just like Mom. 'Run to the store for me, Alicia. The exercise will do you good. Maybe take off a pound or two. *Run,* Alicia!'"

Julie frowned into the sand. But they were right. Alicia looked like . . . what? A whale. Blubbery rubbery. With a lovely face. Minus zits and with fewer chins and pounds, she'd be prettier than Julie.

"Maybe they just want to help."

Alicia snorted. Then, "What on earth can your mother find to nag *you* about?" She looked with distaste at Julie's body. Not one spare milligram of fat, and all the curves in the correct locations.

Julie took a deep breath. "Oh, things." She drew circles in the sand with her forefinger. "Like my jeans being too tight. Like too much eye makeup. Like do I have to play my music so loud. Like getting good *grades* so I'll have an affluent and fulfilling *future.* My *future,* for Pete's sake. I'm fourteen years old. My future's in the future, I say. *Now* is where I happen to be on the 17th of July. Besides . . ." Julie frowned again.

"Besides what?" muttered Alicia into her fat arms.

"Besides," Julie cleared her throat. "The future probably won't even happen."

Alicia raised her head and stared at Julie. She watched her in silence for a few moments. Four gulls were gabbling and squawking at the far end of the beach. The waves were going slap, retreat, slap, retreat, and the sea was icy blue.

"What're you *talking* about? You got some awful disease or something? Like cancer or AIDS, or *what?"* Alicia moved an inch or two farther away.

"No, dopey." *Dumb. Fat and dumb.* "I mean the world killing itself. Dead air. Dead forests. Dead rivers. The Bomb and things." Julie sighed. "Why knock yourself out doing fractions and decimals, and learning irregular verbs, and memorizing history dates, and preparing yourself for a future that's not even going to be *there?*"

"Oh c'mon, Julie. It's gonna be *there.*"

"Huh!" Julie slithered over onto her back and felt the sun's warmth on her face. "Better we should be learning six ways to cook dandelion greens."

"What?"

"Oh, forget it, Alicia. Enjoy the sun." *So much for being alone.*

"Julie!" Stage whisper from The Whale.

"What?"

"Brace yourself." Alicia paused. "I can see the slow approach of Richard Hetherington."

Julie flipped over, so that no one would notice her heart beating in her throat.

"So?"

"So the day has begun. The sun has risen. The beach has blossomed. Flowers are growing in the barren sand."

Julie said nothing. She visualized his arrival. *Eighteen years old.* Shoulders like that Greek statue in the history text. Skinny hips. Long hairy legs. *Voice.* Deep, deep voice, soft and caressing. *I want to touch Richard Hetherington.* She moved against the warm sand and waited.

"Hi." Like a Hammond organ.

"Oh," said Julie, raising herself ever so slowly, ever so casually on one elbow. "Oh," she repeated, "so it's you, Richard. Draw up a towel. Have a piece of sand. Enjoy." *There. I did that very well indeed. Calm and articulate.* She settled down once more upon her arms, face hidden.

"Nice suit," said Richard from somewhere above her.

"What?" This from Alicia.

"Julie's suit," said Richard. "Nice."

"You and Mr. Desmond," sighed Julie. "Two of a kind."

"Meaning?"

Julie looked up. Richard was standing nine feet tall, his head touching the sky.

"Don't ask," said Julie, and buried her face once more on Garfield's flanks.

"Swell day, eh?" offered Alicia.

"What?" Richard frowned, rubbing his ear, as though searching for his hearing aid. "Oh. Yeah. Yeah, swell." He spread his towel beside Julie and lay down close to her, his arm a scant half-inch away. Then their shoulders touched, and he turned to her. "Hi, princess," he grinned.

Julie moved her head and pretended to watch the flight of two cormorants close to the surface of the water. With the change of wind and tide, the surf was higher. The green underbelly of a wave rose, paused; then the water crested, and fell pounding to the sand. Slithering back into itself, the water peaked again and thundered down once more. Julie's breath was coming quickly, as though she were winded from a long run. *Please don't let him hear me breathing. Let me be cool. Let me be in control of this thing.* His finger was moving softly, softly, against her wrist. *If there is a heaven, I am already there.* Then the finger was suddenly still.

Covertly she watched as Richard rose on his elbows and gazed down the beach. His light blue pupils, circled by dark rims, scanned the scene – like Paul Newman's eyes from a 70's movie – and suddenly rivetted on something.

Then, "I give you a report," he said, voice rumbling. There was a pause. "The Body approaches," he went on, "in company with two familiar fillies. Trailing behind this small parade are three lovestruck gentlemen, all of our acquaintance."

Julie's head rose carefully, painfully. Alicia was already focussed on the group.

"The Body . . ?" began Julie uncertainly.

Richard interrupted. "I think one may assume that The Body belongs to Virginia's cousin from Boston. An American Body, in short. On a month-long visit, I am told – if one may dare to believe such a miracle of good fortune. I rise," he announced, unfolding himself in one slow, sure movement, "to offer an official Canadian welcome." He sauntered, long-legged and lithe, towards the group.

Julie turned to Alicia, suddenly becoming a dear and comforting ally.

"Well damnit all, anyway," she said to Alicia, who replied, "Yes."

The Body was indeed someone to welcome on behalf of any nation. Ash blonde hair tossed in the wind, a creamy tan, tall and oppressively graceful. A slick Siamese among kittens and tabby cats.

"There goes my summer," said Julie.

"I'm going on a diet," groaned Alicia. "This afternoon. This morning. Yesterday. At least he called you 'princess'."

"That was *before,*" said Julie.

"Don't complain. All he said to me was 'What?' Y'got to admit that 'Hi, princess' is an improvement on *that.*"

Within minutes, the air was filled with music from Ted's ghetto blaster. Jim was dancing with Virginia, and Richard Hetherington was chasing The Body into the icy cold water. Mr. Desmond passed by, frowning. Julie and Alicia laughed a lot, danced, duck-dived through the waves, applied baby oil to skin that was already slippery as butter, exchanged agonized glances.

"I suppose," said Julie to Alicia as they parted at Julie's cottage at noon, "that I really shouldn't mind this so much. After all, beside him, I'm only a two-bit kid. It's just that it seemed kind of close. I could feel him *scanning* me. He *touched* me, Alicia."

"Well," sighed Alicia, panting from her walk up the hill, "he sure didn't scan *me*. Or touch me. He'd probably *recoil* if he touched me." She fiddled with the strap on her beach bag. "Lookit, Julie. This is the way I figure about guys like Richard."

"What? What do you figure?"

"I figure they're for decoration. For smartening up the beach. For night-time daydreams. He's supposed to be real hot material. Julie?" She paused.

"Yeah?"

Alicia bit her lip. "I don't think you're ready."

"Well, I sure *feel* ready."

"Yeah. Well, you're *not.*"

"Well . . . *maybe*. Maybe not for the really heavy manoeuvres."

"So let's leave him to The Body, and just try to enjoy the performance."

Julie surveyed The Whale. Probably you could afford to be philosophical when you were without hope of any kind.

"I suppose in the future . . ." she began.

"What future?" Alicia grinned, and her pretty face was bright with amusement. "I thought there wasn't going to be any future."

Julie laughed. "Well," she said, "There's always two ways of looking at everything. 'Bye now. See you this afternoon."

She ran down the path to the stairway of her veranda, where her mother was sweeping the steps.

"Hi, Mom!" she said, and gave her mother a swift kiss on the cheek. "Love ya."

"Me too," said her mother. "Don't track all that sand in over my clean floors." Lightly she touched the side of Julie's face. "Was it fun on the beach today?" she asked.

HAIR

Lois Simmie

My grandma says everyone has a cross to bear and I know for a fact she's right. Mine is hair. Not just my hair, my friends' hair, too – and that adds up to at least three crosses, or maybe just different parts of the same one.

I'd like to say right away that I'm not a jealous person; jealousy is such a crummy emotion, like self-pity, so I try hard not to have it, and that's probably good for my soul or something. It's probably *character building* to have two friends and a brother with absolutely gorgeous hair while yours is wispy and straight and looks like rats were chewing on it while you were asleep. With all this character building, I'll probably end up a saint or something. Saint Darcy.

And people will collect clippings of my hair and fingernails, and they'll look at the hair and say: poor thing, she'd *have* to be a saint to live with hair like that.

The friends are Kim and Tracy and it's not their fault they have this incredible hair – thick, bouncy, shiny *and* curly. Kim's is blonde and Tracy's is black. At least they don't fling it around under your nose and moan about not being able to do a thing with it – like some of the girls in the school washroom – and they both say they'd trade their hair for my eyes any day. They are my best feature, the only one (or should I say two) worth mentioning, bright turquoise with long eyelashes. They probably wouldn't trade really, but it helps some when they say it. My brother Dan has dark curly hair, and the same eyes, only longer eyelashes. I like him anyway. Most of the time.

Not only is my hair a mangy, dusty brown, sort of like an old fur coat forgotten in somebody's attic, it is also mean. You hear about people abusing their hair – too much bleach and stuff – but you never hear about hair that abuses *you*. Malicious, *diabolical* hair. Kim and Tracy used to try to do something about my hair but they've given up – they know now what they're up against.

"I could give you a perm," Kim said last summer as we sat and dried off by the George Ward pool. Neither of our folks are rich enough to have a pool, so we always swim with about a thousand screaming little kids who cannonball into you and splash you evilly when you're trying not to get wet. I love to swim but I hate getting wet. Kim's hair was cut short and popping up in sunshiny curls all over the place, while mine dripped malevolently down my neck and in my eyes.

"I gave Treena a perm and it looks terrific," Kim said. Her sister Treena has straight hair, but thick and blonde like Kim's.

"Mmmm, I don't know. Mom says my hair wouldn't take a perm, it'd get all frizzy and fall out or something."

"I'd be real careful. You just don't leave the solution on as long," she said, stretching out to tan herself. She really sounded like she knew what she was talking about.

"I'll think about it," I said, starting to feel excited about the idea. Some screeching boys came tearing past, spraying water on Kim's back.

"Get lost!" she yelled. Kim is going to be a teacher.

Mom didn't think it was a good idea but she said if I bought the perm with my own money there wasn't much she could say, but "don't say I didn't warn you." Don't you love it when people say that? So I bought it that night, and a "Sunny Blonde" colour rinse I saw when I was picking out the perm. Sunny blonde. I went straight home and put it on my hair, but it didn't do a thing except make me $3.69 plus tax poorer.

We did the perm at the picnic table in the yard because Mom didn't want the smell in the house. Kim rolled my hair with the same look of concentration she gets when she's going for a lay-up in the gym. Our dog, Doc, sat looking at me with his head cocked on one side like he was trying to decide how I would look with curly hair.

"Your hair is a lot harder to roll than Treena's," Kim said, frowning and rolling a curler for the third time. "It doesn't co-operate."

"Yeah, well, I've got mean hair. I keep trying to tell you."

"That's what it *used* to be like," Kim said confidently, which set me to fantasizing about the new me, with this soft halo of curls – shiny, thick, bouncy and, unaccountably, a beautiful shade of blonde. Sunny blonde. How Jake Turner, the hottest guy in school would suddenly *see* me... *"Well, well, we... ll. And when did* YOU *arrive at our fair school?"*

I looked in the hand mirror. I looked skinned and pale with a humungous red zit on the end of my nose. Like a big drowned mouse, sort of.

"There," Kim said, reaching for the curl paper I held out and wrestling the last curler into place. She sounded like someone who's just finished digging a hundred-foot ditch.

"We'll put the solution on and I'll do a test curl in five minutes." Then she soaked each curl with this evil-smelling stuff while I held an old towel up to my face. The stuff dripped into my ears. "I don't want curly hair in my ears," I said. I was starting to get nervous. Doc disappeared under the lilac bush and covered his nose with his paws.

Then she got us a Coke and we drank it, with Kim watching the time like a hawk. I tried to go back to the fantasy but the zit kept getting in the way.

"Five minutes. Time for the test curl. Better safe than sorry," Kim chimed out like a dementedly cheerful hairdresser, and she unrolled a curler. She screamed and ran in the house.

I grabbed the mirror. A slimy green snail stuck to my scalp. I screamed. Mom came running out. She screamed. Dan skidded around the corner of the house. "Help, help! An alien!" Kim ran back out, looked again and burst into tears. Doc tore around, barking like crazy, and Mrs. Mazca, our neighbour, peered over the hedge. I grabbed the hose and sprayed my head, screeching and clawing at the curlers with Kim trying to get close enough to help. We both got soaked and I surfaced with my whole head covered with green snails that dried into an explosion of brassy greenish frizz. Like I was wearing a big Brillo pot cleaner on my head, or I'd stuck my finger in a light socket – which I would have if I'd thought of it.

First I cried and so did Kim. Then we laughed till we cried. Then we laughed and cried some more. I barely survived the experience.

Mr. Paulson, our English teacher, asked us to write a poem about something that really bothered us a lot and if we didn't want to read it in class we didn't have to. We didn't even have to hand it in, just tell him we'd done it. Mr. Paulson is so cool.

Almost everybody wrote about really big scary things like war and child abuse and suicide, and I wrote about hair. I wasn't going to read it until Todd read his poem called "Love Sucks", all about girls who say when you break up we'll always be friends and then you never see them again, and how he'd rather have gangrene crawling up his leg than be in love, and it was really funny, but you could tell the way people laughed they were laughing with him, not at him. So I read my poem. They laughed when I read "Kim's is long and blonde and wavy, Mine is straight and coloured gravy," and the line about my mom saying it didn't matter but all I want is hair that's fatter. They all knew about fat hair. Somehow it helped.

But no poem is going to help the way I feel about what happened at the dance.

I was grown back to the mangy, rat-chewed look that almost made me miss the wild green hair which at least, once I was used to it, gave me a kind of distinctive look. I'd convinced myself it didn't even look that weird with other kids dying their hair orange and purple and shaving it off in strips. At least it had *body.* After that my own hair looked prim. Can you think of anything worse than prim hair?

Todd, the one who wrote the "Love Sucks" poem, asked me to the dance, which really surprised me. It was going to be extra special, the last one of the school year with lots of decorations and music by Killer Leeches, a really cool group from across town. And I liked Todd. Besides being nice, and funny, he is also tall and an awesome dancer. I may as well admit my only other real date was with a guy who smoked and bit his nails till they bled and accidentally set the Pizza Hut menu on fire. But I was pretty comfortable with Todd, who sits next to me in biology class and always makes me laugh. The only thing to worry about was what to do with my hair.

"Never mind your damned hair," Mom said. My mother can be quite callous about my problem. "Todd asked you with your hair just the way it is." Grandma understands, since I got stuck with her hair genes. My Uncle Dan says he didn't recognize Grandma at his wedding because she wasn't in curlers. She worked nights in a bakery for years and spent every day in curlers just to work in the back of the bakery in a hairnet with one other woman. A lot of people wouldn't understand that, but I do.

I really wanted to look good for that dance.

"We could try crimping your hair, Darcy," Tracy said. "We'll do it a couple of times before the dance to see how it works out."

"It's no use. My hair will do something awful."

"No, it won't. What can it do? It will either crimp or it won't, and that's that." She eyed my flat hair. "Give it some body."

She had used the magic word. "Okay," I said.

It was a miracle, no other word for it. It looked just fabulous, with lots of energy and a kind of nice vagabond look to it, like I'd been too busy climbing mountains and hang-gliding to bother about it. It had a kind of wind-whipped look and, oh, eighth wonder of the world, it had BODY. Lots and lots of body.

All *right.* I rushed out and bought some dangly earrings, which I'd never been able to wear, and started tossing my head experimentally around like the girls in the shampoo ads looking up at those guys who you know wouldn't give the time of day to somebody with prim hair.

Tracy crimped it twice before the dance just to make sure it was going to work. It did. It even stayed crimped all one afternoon while I shopped for a dress. I was in heaven.

Todd apologized for not having a car. His brother needed his car, and he said he'd feel like a geek driving his dad's Chrysler. I didn't care and it was so nice out that night we just walked to the dance.

"We'll get a cab home," Todd said. He really was tall when you walked beside him. Todd has a kind of springy walk, as if any moment he might start to dance like the people in those old musicals my folks always watch.

"It doesn't matter," I said. "We can maybe catch a ride with Kim and Ryan."

"You look great, Darcy," Todd said, looking at me like he really meant it. "I like your hair that way."

"Oh, really? Thanks," I said, tossing it a bit as if to say, "This old stuff?" Nobody, but *nobody* had ever said that to me in my entire life.

"I like yours, too," I said. "At least it isn't curly." And he laughed. Todd has a nice laugh.

"Yeah, that was a cool poem," he said.

"Thanks. So was yours. Especially the gangrene part."

"Yeah. I kind of liked that, too. I'm going to be a writer."

"No kidding. Me, too." As soon as I said it I knew it was true.

"Hey, you know what? Maybe we could get together and read our stuff to each other before we give it to Mr. Paulson."

"That's a great idea," I said. "Then it wouldn't be so hard to do it in front of the class."

"Right," he said, looking happy. "How about Mondays after dinner, and then there'd be time to make changes if we want."

"Sure. That's a good time for me."

The gym looked great, with hundreds of white and purple balloons (our school colours), and streamers, and soft coloured lights, and it didn't even smell too sweaty. It was really hot in there though – they'd always had a heat problem, which accounted for the sweaty smell and people falling over like trees in the middle of volleyball games – and I was glad my cotton dress was cool and cut low in the back. We'd wanted to have the dance someplace else but couldn't afford it, so big fans were set up all over the place which felt really good when you danced by. The air lifted my bounteous hair and it felt wonderful. Killer Leeches was really cool, as good as everybody'd said, and the gym was jumping in no time.

I'd danced with Todd at a couple of house parties and knew he was good but not how good; he was so good he made you look good, if you know what I mean. The first couple of hours just vanished like smoke, and I didn't want them to because I'd never, but never, had such a good time. I danced every dance – lots but not all with Todd – while the gym got hotter and hotter, and I thought: thank God for the man who invented deodorant, he should have a day named after him or something. I even danced with Jake Turner and surreptitiously pinched myself, but I wasn't dreaming.

"You're a great dancer," Jake said.

"Thanks," I said, looking up at him and tossing my head. I'd been forgetting to do my shampoo commercial thing.

"Yeah. You and Todd are awesome together."

Holy cow. I couldn't believe my ears. I was glad the music was so loud I didn't have to answer. Where had I been all these years? This was living with a capital L.

Until I went to the washroom. Practically danced into the washroom and saw myself in the mirror.

I clutched the edge of the sink, like a heroine in a silent movie confronted by a villain, and stared. My hair was straight. It was straight, limp, mangy, mousy, flat. It was prim. Not a trace of a crimp, wave, curl was left, not even a slight bend anywhere. Straight. My nose shone like a beacon, my lipstick was gone, and most of my mascara was under my eyes. I burst into tears.

"Are you okay, Darcy?" Todd asked when I finally returned.

"Take me home," I said.

"What?"

"I want to go home."

"Why? Are you sick?"

"No. I just want to go home."

So he got my sweater and his jacket and we left.

We went outside and started to walk home. I couldn't talk.

"Did I do something wrong?" he asked.

"No."

"Can't you tell me what's wrong?"

"No."

"I thought maybe you felt sick from the heat in there. Some people were feeling like that."

I didn't answer.

Just then the Number 6 bus came by and we got on and rode home in silence. I saw my reflection once in the bus window and wished I hadn't. With my puffy eyes and limp hair, I looked like a forty-year-old cleaning woman riding the bus home after a hard day's work.

At my stop we got off and Todd walked me to the door.

"Goodnight," I said.

But he just shrugged and walked away.

Well, that was Friday night and I've just spent the worst weekend of my life. I feel like such a fool every time I think about it (which is almost all the time), tossing my head around like that and thinking I looked so great when I looked like . . . that. Like me. I lay on my bed and stared at my horse collection on the shelf, wishing I was ten years old again.

The worst of it is what to do about Todd. I really like him, you know. Quite a bit, I mean. But how do you explain such a stupid thing to anybody? I was having such a wonderful time before I looked in the mirror and I must have looked exactly the same before as after but everything changed. Well, it was me that changed, I guess. And I keep thinking about what Mom said about Todd liking me well enough with my mangy old hair to ask me in the first place.

It's tomorrow night we were supposed to meet and go over our stuff for Mr. Paulson's class and I haven't written anything yet. Of course Todd won't want to have anything more to do with such a mental case, but I've got to explain it to him somehow – how I felt. Maybe I'll just give him this to read. I think I will. It can't be any worse than trying to explain it.

And who needs curly hair anyway? I'm shaving it off like Sinead O'Connor's, and that's that.

MY CURRENT OBSESSION

Jocelyn Shipley

My friend Emma says obsessions are bad. She says being obsessed with a guy is the worst, really weak and negative, and it can wreck your life. But she's wrong. My obsession with Madhar is good for me. For one thing, I've stopped thinking about losing weight all the time. For another, I've stopped caring about dumb blonde jokes, which used to reduce me to tears. I barely even notice now when someone calls me *Daffy,* instead of Daphne, and I don't even care when they make fun of synchro. So really, I'd say there's a lot of strength in my current obsession. I'd say Emma's the crazy one.

Speaking of Madhar, let me tell you about him. He's so cool! Not exactly handsome, but goodlooking in an interesting, exotic kind of way. He's a loner (just like me) – if he ever hangs out it's with one or two other guys, not a big group. He's tall, slender, smooth-looking. He runs like a jaguar. When I told Emma that, about the jaguar, she said it was pathetically trite. But who cares? Love is trite, and I am in love.

I cut Madhar's picture (which shows off so perfectly his even white teeth against his dark skin and hair) out of the Northington High yearbook and put it in my locket, which I wear all the time, except in the water. (I wrap it up in my underwear in the change room.) I stole the piece of chalk he wrote on the blackboard with the day I realized I loved him. When I lie in bed at night (his chalk under my pillow), I chant his name, *Madhar Ramanan, Madhar Ramanan, Madhar Ramanan,* over and over and over as I fall asleep. I've also stopped mentioning him to Emma. I want him all to myself.

Now I'll tell you about me. I'm a big, strapping girl, my Uncle Frazer says. *Buxom,* he says. Mom rolled her eyes at that, and I had to go look it up – I never look up any of the other old-fashioned words my uncle uses, but when it applied to me, to how I look, well, I just had to know.

Buxom means "plump and good to look at", also "healthy and cheerful", also "lively and frolicsome." It's a word that's only used to describe females, I learned. Oh. So men are not *buxom*. Somehow, no matter what the dictionary says, I get the idea the word *buxom* makes people think of breasts.

I overheard Mom lecturing Uncle Frazer in the kitchen. "Don't say things like that to her. She's self-conscious enough as it is." But my mother is wrong too. I got over feeling mortified by my big boobs ages ago. I mean, the year I was twelve was hell, and even last winter I thought I might go through life eternally embarrassed. But since meeting Madhar I have much more important things to think about.

Anyway, last September I joined the Northington Mermaids, a competitive synchronized swim club. Emma thinks it's hilarious. I'll admit, it's a dopey name, but she says the stupidest things about synchro – a lot of people do – without having the first clue. She's no idea how hard our workouts are. And there's no way she could hang upside down under water like we do, holding for a full eight counts, toes so pointed they cramp, sculling like mad to keep from travelling.

I lost a lot of weight last year, swimming six hours a week, and I wasn't about to flab up again when the Mermaids finished for the summer. So I took this job driving a Dairy Delite Ice Cream cart. Pedalling trims the tummy and slims the thighs, my coach Brigitte says. Of course the thought of earning some cash for a whole new wardrobe was pretty tempting too. (I plan to do Grade 11 in style.)

I really had no idea this job would feed my obsession with Madhar. That was a complete bonus. Since school was over in June I thought I'd go crazy, daydreaming about him all the time but never seeing him. I didn't know how I was going to survive for two whole months. So when I started my route, which takes me to Northington Park in the evenings, and found out he plays soccer there almost every night, I just couldn't believe it.

I was so excited I was even civil to Uncle Frazer for a few days! Which is pretty amazing, considering how much he bugs me. I don't want anything to do with him, but he's kind of hard to avoid, since he's staying with us for the summer. He's my mother's older brother, and she hasn't seen him in about ten years, because he lives in England. He's doing research at U. of T. – something about medieval manuscripts. He's not married or anything. I feel really mean not being nicer to him, but he kind of scares me. He's so weird! And I'm so afraid it will rub off on me.

Here's an example of how weird he is. Every Christmas and birthday he sends me a silver spoon. Other kids' relatives give them money or music or clothes, but Uncle Frazer gives me spoons. They're all displayed on a wooden rack, shaped like a map of Canada, in my room. Actually, I like them quite a lot – most of them are antique, and they're all from different places. Some are even engraved with initials or a name. It's just that spoons are such a strange thing to give a kid.

And then he talks funny too. He's always using odd words and phrases I don't understand. Sometimes he sounds sort of like a textbook; other times, usually after he's been into the wine, he sounds like someone from the fourteenth century, saying things like *buxom* or *wench* or *chaste*. When he talks like that he giggles a lot and plays with his beard, which is quite reddish, although his hair, what he's got left, is a dull greyish-brown.

Driving the Dairy Delite cart is totally boring in the afternoons. Our subdivision is called Forest Glen, although there's not a mature tree in sight. Just houses and sidewalks and sprinklers. And every few blocks a superbox, which is what we have instead of home delivery for mail. Forest Glen is built around a golf course though, so there's sometimes a view of the greens, as if that would help. Most days it's stifling, sweating hot. Even if there's a breeze it's like a dust storm, because of new construction to the west.

Up and down the streets I roam, like the Pied Piper, except instead of playing a merry tune I get to ring the silly kindergarten bell on my handlebar. All the little kids come running, calling, begging. "Please, Daphne, oh please, please, please." But of course I can't give anything away free – that would cut into my profits. So I take their money for my rip-off Arctic Pops and Frosty Bars and think about the new fall clothes already in the stores up at the mall (there's a navy blue turtleneck I'm going to get, to complement my eyes), and wonder whether I'll have any classes with Madhar first semester, and if I do, will he remember me?

Most days I ride by Emma's house – she works at MacDonald's, but only evenings, so she's usually home and bored silly. She comes out and talks to me while we eat a Dairy Delite Bar (low-fat, low-cal), and sip from the bottle of filtered water I always carry with me. She goes on and on about kids and clothes and stuff, but I barely even listen anymore. I just think about Madhar.

I count the minutes until about five o'clock, when sales slack off (there's a time just before dinner when most parents won't buy their kids Dairy Delite junk). Then I head home to eat and shower and put on clean clothes. To kill some time I mess around with my hair, which I grew long this year (even my bangs) for synchro. It always bleaches out in the summer, and because I've got such a good tan from being outside all day, it looks even blonder. I don't wear any makeup, except for a bit of lipstick called Roseberry.

Then I drive my cart up to the park behind our house, where the arena, pool, tennis courts, baseball diamonds, and soccer pitches are. Besides the mall it's the place for kids to hang out, so there's always something going on and it's always fun. I do my route so that I end up on the hill overlooking the soccer pitch where Madhar plays. He's on the Northington rep team, which practices on Tuesdays and has a home game on Thursdays. (He's the best!) On the other nights, when he's not playing out of town, he referees little kids' games.

I'd never admit this to my mother, but now I'm glad she made me sign up for enriched math, or I might never have met Madhar. Mom's an accountant and thinks math is the most important subject I can take. We had a big fight (which she won) about whether I should settle for an easy A in a regular class, or work harder, learn more, and maybe get only a B in enriched. At first that class really bugged me. Everyone in it acted like they were the most brilliant beings on earth. Except for Madhar. He was always quiet, never trying to be smarter than the teacher, never showing off by arguing a point to death, never groaning when I asked a stupid question. Then he got a perfect score on a national contest we had to write, and everybody started saying he's a genius.

I fell in love with him on May 7, when he was up at the blackboard solving a problem nobody else could do. How I could have gone to that class every single day all semester and never really appreciated him before I just don't know. He worked with such style and confidence. And so fast! When he explained what he'd written out, his voice did something heavenly to me. My whole body went limp. Not jellyfish limp, like when I was fat, but just very relaxed and mellow, like after swimming fifty lengths.

Once the teacher asked him to help me with some equations, and I thought I might faint when he sat down next to me. There was a delicious, spicy smell to him (not at all like that sickening aftershave some guys wear), and as we worked I felt a kind of aura of sensitive intelligence surrounding him. (What makes me think Emma would laugh at that too?)

Soccer is something I've never really cared about before. I hate running. It makes me wheeze. But watching Madhar play and referee makes soccer seem like the most exciting game ever. I go into secret raptures about the way he looks in his rep uniform – white shorts with high red socks that show off his knees and thigh muscles, red shirt with Northington and a big number 15 in white on the back. Fifteen. My age exactly. I wonder if that's significant?

When I get home I spend my time wondering where he is and what he's doing. Is he watching the Jays on TV like my mother? Is he working alone in his room with his books, like Uncle Frazer? Is he lying in his room as darkness comes, thinking about someone special, like I am?

I've never really had heaps of boyfriends like Emma does. Okay, I've never really had a boyfriend, period. Sometimes I think I never will.

Uncle Frazer always teases me about guys, which just makes me feel worse. As if he could talk – forty-five years old and still single. Scary!

Most girls make a plan when they like a guy, but I don't have any idea what to do. Sure, I long to talk to Madhar and spend time with him, but I have no idea how to get started. I don't phone him, I don't go up to him after a game. I just sort of live with the idea of him.

I really wish I could discuss this with Emma, but I'm afraid she'd mock me. She's so sarcastic sometimes. I know she'd tell me to give it up, which I'm absolutely not going to do. She'd probably call Madhar a geek. And she'd definitely call me a loser.

It's almost the end of August and I'm watching Madhar referee, wondering if he knows I sell my Nice 'n Nutty Bars and my Double Chocolate Delights in this particular spot every night just to be near him. Then suddenly the coach of the losing team gets all worked up over a call, and starts yelling and screaming at Madhar. I've seen lots of disagreements in these games, but this is much nastier. Maybe it's because of the intense heat and humidity we've had all week. Maybe it's the pressure of the playoffs. It's something about a goal not counting because a player was offside, and soon the other coach and a lot of parents are in on it too.

Madhar stands calmly in the centre. He keeps shaking his head and holding out his lean brown arms. The losing coach puts on a big show, roaring and swearing, insulting everyone in sight. Most of the parents start dragging their kids away, calling, "Forget it, let's finish the game." But this coach just gets more worked up, his face going purple with rage. Finally Madhar throws him out.

There's silence. What will Madhar do if he refuses to go? But then the parents turn on the guy, yelling, "Yeah . . . get lost . . . bad example . . . the ref's right," and things like that. I sigh with relief as he stomps away.

But that's not the end of it. At the top of the slope which separates the field from the parking lot he turns and yells, "Why don'tcha go back where ya come from, ya stinkin' Paki?"

Madhar doesn't react at all. He simply blows his whistle for the game to begin again. I pedal quickly away, as embarrassed as if I'd said it myself. I know some kids at school think like that, but most of them wouldn't dare say it, let alone shout it. I feel ashamed, sort of hot and blushing like I do when guys make rude remarks about my breasts.

I lie awake a long time in the sticky, breathless air, staring at my silver spoons in their Canada map rack, and thinking about Madhar. I want to tell him I don't care where he comes from, I just love him, but I can't figure out how. I can't just walk up to him tomorrow and say something like that.

And then it comes to me that I should give him something. But what? A note? No, that's too obvious. It would have to be something more significant. As I fall asleep I have the absurd idea to give him one of my silver spoons.

The next morning I choose one. It only seems right it should be my favourite, if it's to be as meaningful as I intend. My favourite is also the smallest, no longer than the width of my hand. A tiny maple leaf with slightly curled edges forms the bowl; a tiny beaver tops the handle, on which *Canada* is engraved. The word *sterling* is stamped on the back. It seems an appropriate, symbolic gift for Madhar, and I drop it down the front of my T-shirt into my bra.

I wear Madhar's spoon there over my heart all day, wondering how to get up the nerve to give it to him. You might think it would be uncomfortable, but it isn't. The spoon is so small, it just settles in under my breast like it belongs there.

As I watch Madhar's game I can feel the spoon, silvery-cool against my warm body, the tiny curled edges of the leaf-bowl sort of tickling me. I feel like I'm preparing some kind of charm for him, as if the combination of a sterling silver spoon from Canada, my sweat, and my hopeful heartbeats could cast a spell that would make him love me. When it's over I wait at the top of the slope where I can see the car that always comes for him. Tonight a young woman (perhaps his sister?) is driving.

Hoping no one will notice, I pull out the spoon, holding it tightly, willing it to work magic for me. As Madhar jogs towards the parking lot, I'm more nervous than I've ever been, even before swimming in competition. I have that awful feeling of sitting on the edge of the pool, ready, tense, waiting for the music to start.

Madhar, his straight dark hair a bit wild from running, looks towards me, but quickly (shyly?) looks away. He's wearing his ref's uniform tonight – short black shorts, high black socks, black and white striped shirt. Oh, the sight of him!

"Madhar!" I call, without really knowing I was going to. It's as if the music has started and I'm automatically diving into the water to begin my routine. I climb off my Dairy Delite cart and sort of run towards him. "Hi! It's me, Daphne. From math class?"

Madhar glances over at the young woman, who has gotten out of the car and is standing on the slope too. She's dressed in a sari, shades of peacock blue and scarlet, and her hair, as dark and thick as Madhar's, hangs almost to her waist. She stares coldly at me. Madhar gives me a curt little wave and keeps going.

I panic. Now it's as if someone has made a mistake and started the wrong music, as sometimes happens. The beat is all wrong, my moves are off, I'm totally out of synch. There is something in the look that woman is giving me that tells me without a doubt it would be a mistake to give my silver spoon to Madhar.

I jump back on my cart, not very gracefully, and head for home on my oversized tricycle. I'm trembling, and I realize I've come very close to doing something quite bizarre. What was I thinking of? How could I have imagined Madhar would want my stupid spoon, even if it was sterling silver and from Canada? What did I think he was going to say? "Hey, you big brilliant babe, let's do math together?" What a fool I was!

If Uncle Frazer is home when I get there, and if he says one single word about guys to me, I'm going to blast him like I should have done weeks ago. I'm going to scream at him to *get a life!* Then I'm going to take Madhar's picture out of my locket, and his chalk from under my pillow, and flush both down the toilet so I can never, ever get them back.

Then I'm going to call Emma and tell her everything.

THE IMPORTANCE OF BEING BRACKNELL

Joanne Findon

I never thought I'd have to admit to throwing a pizza at my director or spilling coffee all over my best friend. I also never thought I'd manage to get Pete's eyes off Charmaine for more than five seconds. But it's been a bizarre week.

I'm in this play at school. It's called *The Importance of Being Earnest,* written by some English guy about a hundred years ago. It's pretty funny, actually. Anyways, I had been thinking about joining the drama club for a long time, but I figured I was too shy to do anything like that. Then my best friend Charmaine told me that Pete Burwell was going to be in it. Pete Burwell is *to die for.* I've liked him secretly for years. He has a cute chuckly laugh that always gives me the shivers.

So I auditioned. That was pretty horrible. I wanted to be Gwendolyn or Cecily – they're the two beautiful young women who end up marrying men who both call themselves Ernest. (It's a long story.) But I knew I didn't stand a chance when Charmaine read the part of Gwendolyn and tossed her cloud of golden hair at our director, Robert (a Grade 12 guy who's had the hots for her for years). And then in swooshed Erin Demchuk with her enormous, astonished green eyes to audition for Cecily. Needless to say, she got the part.

So guess what was left for me.

"You'll be a *great* Lady Bracknell, Lena," said Robert, frowning his serious Director Frown at me. Robert fancies himself the Next Great Canadian Director and never loses a chance to let everyone know just what his glorious destiny is.

"But I don't *want* to be Lady Bracknell," I said. "She's such a . . . a . . ."

"A 'gorgon', as Jack says. Yes, but think of the creative possibilities! It's a great character part, Lena! Believe me, there are some in the Theatre who would *kill* for a part like Lady Bracknell."

I scowled at him. A great character part. I could see my future on the stage stretching out ahead of me. Hags and gum-snapping waitresses and eccentric neighbours.

I sighed, and gave in.

"Okay," I said. At least I'd be seeing Pete at rehearsals. Maybe if I turned in a convincing Lady Bracknell, he'd notice that there's more to me than good marks in French.

"Oh, thank you!" Robert exclaimed, grabbing my shoulders and kissing me on each cheek like they do in France. "You won't regret it! You'll be brilliant!"

"Yeah, you'll be great, really!" said Charmaine, squeezing my arm like a real friend.

I glanced at Pete, but his eyes were on Charmaine. My heart sank.

We started rehearsing after school. Actually, Lady Bracknell wasn't so bad. It felt good to be able to order people around without having to face the consequences. And I love it when she says things like: "To lose one parent may be regarded as a misfortune; to lose both looks like carelessness." Charmaine taught me how to hold my chin up in the air and look down on everyone else (even if they were taller than me), and how to talk in a deep, haughty voice. I even started ordering my brother around the house just for practice. Mom thought this was a result of getting home late for dinner, but I didn't see it that way then. After a couple of weeks I thought I had the character down pat.

There was something else about it too. In the play, Lady Bracknell tries to stop her daughter Gwendolyn from marrying this guy Jack, whose name is really Ernest, but who doesn't know it until the very end, and who doesn't have any parents because he was found in a handbag in Victoria Station when he was a baby (did I mention that it's a long story?) At the same time, Jack (or Ernest) tries to stop Algernon, Lady Bracknell's nephew, from marrying Cecily, Jack's young ward. It's all very complicated. Anyways, because Peter was Jack and Charmaine was Gwendolyn I could object all I wanted to them getting together, because it's all in the script, if you see what I mean. So I could say what I meant without really saying what I meant. Of course it didn't work out so well for Robert, who aside from directing was also playing Algernon. Robert isn't interested in Erin, only in Charmaine.

At last we were ready to have a dress rehearsal on the stage in the gym. Robert got the key to the store-room from the office and we all trooped in there to pick out costumes.

The room was stuffed with clothes hung on rows and rows of metal rods.

"Look at this!" said Charmaine, pulling a pink taffeta thing off the hanger and holding it up to herself.

"And here's just the thing for you, Lena," said Pete, pulling down a huge golden brocade dress with puffy arms and a knot of material at the back that I think was supposed to be a bustle.

"An August gown for Aunt Augusta," trilled Robert in his most theatrical voice.

I stared at it. I knew Pete wasn't exactly swooning over me, but did he actually hate me?

"It's awful," I said. "I won't wear it. It's hideous."

"Remember, Lena. You are Augusta Bracknell, chief Gorgon of the 19th Century Stage," said Robert. "You're supposed to look hideous."

"Thanks."

"Give it a chance, Lena," said Charmaine. "With your hair piled up and some makeup, you'll look really regal and imposing."

"Humph," I said, crossing my arms and glaring at them all. "I look bilious in yellow. Can't we find something else?"

"The biliouser the better!" shouted Robert.

I knew I had lost.

It was four-thirty by the time we all had on our costumes and makeup. Charmaine had put big blotches of red rouge on my cheeks, well below the cheekbones.

"This makes you look older," she explained. "Older women get hollow-cheeked – this makes it more convincing."

I tried not to glare at her in the mirror, but it wasn't easy.

When we were all on stage and Brent, the lighting guy, had flashed all the different coloured lights on and off a few times, we *finally* started the rehearsal. I had to admit that everyone looked pretty good. Pete and Robert were very smart in their black waistcoats. Charmaine had her hair in ringlets and swished around gracefully in that pink dress. Erin was wide-eyed in a gown of sea green with a big bow at the waist that made her look like an overgrown little girl – which is what she's supposed to look like, I guess.

And I . . . well . . .

"You look magnificently awful," Pete chuckled at me. He was grinning, so I didn't feel so bad.

"Why, thank you," I said, pointing my nose in the air and looking down at him.

But when we started the rehearsal, things didn't go so well.

Robert kept forgetting his lines. Drew Smithers, who was playing one of the butlers, managed to drop the teapot on Erin's foot; she stormed out and Charmaine had to drag her back. Robert kept yelling "Cut, cut!" and making us begin the scene again when anyone did anything wrong.

By the time we'd started the last scene for the fifth time it was seven o'clock. My stomach was growling and I was more tired and fed up than I had been for a long time. When my turn came to confront Miss Prism, I shouted "Prism! *Where is that baby?*" so loudly at poor Winona Baker that she looked like she was about to burst into tears.

"Brilliant! Brilliant!" exclaimed Robert, dancing up and down.

"Just get on with it," said Pete out of the corner of his mouth.

I ranted on and finished my speech, and somehow Winona pulled herself together and answered. We all finished the scene and the play was over.

"That's it," I said, sweeping across the stage toward the change rooms. "That's enough for today. I'm starved."

"No, I want to do that last scene one more time." said Robert. "Take it from where Lady Bracknell enters. Lena?"

I spun on my heel and walked right up to Robert. I faced him, nose to nose.

"I take it you didn't hear me correctly, Robert. I said no. That is enough for today."

His mouth fell open. I heard Charmaine giggle behind me. Erin was already swishing off to the girls' changing room.

"Let's go for pizza," said Pete. I glanced at him, and he gave me a wink.

I looked back at Robert, whose mouth was still open. I reached out and with one finger gently pushed his chin up to shut it. Then I turned and walked past him after the others.

Inside the changing room Charmaine was glowing.

"I can't believe you stood up to him, Lena! Nobody's ever done that before!"

"I don't know. It wasn't that hard." I scrubbed at the heavy stage makeup. "I just wanted to get out of there."

"It must be the role, Lena," she laughed. "Bracknell is getting into your blood."

"Yeah." A lot of good it'll do me, I thought.

Charmaine was so excited at seeing Robert get his own back that she took longer than usual to change. Erin and the others had left. I was leaning on the door waiting for her when I first felt strange. The rush I'd had when I got mad at Robert was long gone and I felt like I hadn't slept for a week.

"Let's go!" I said, trying not to sound as grumpy as I felt.

"Okay, okay!" Charmaine grabbed her purse, *finally,* and headed my way.

The guys were out beside Pete's beat-up Toyota. Robert was deep in conversation with Drew, and Pete was looking bored. He perked up when he saw us, or more correctly, when he saw Charmaine.

"Let's go," I said, brushing past Robert and flinging my bag into the back seat.

He looked for a second like he was about to protest, but then he saw me glaring at him.

"Hey, see you tomorrow," he said to Drew. Drew waved and Robert got in with the rest of us.

It was a quarter to eight by the time we got to the pizza place. It was pretty busy, but we got a table in a couple of minutes.

At last! I looked hungrily at the menu.

"I guess we'll have our usual two mediums?" said Robert, raising one eyebrow artfully.

"Sure, whatever," said Pete.

"No," I said. "I'm starving. I'm going to order a small for myself."

"Now, Lena," said Robert, leaning forward with that "Let's be reasonable" look on his face. "You know it always works better this way because then we can order two with different toppings."

I looked at him. Suddenly a huge, unreasoning anger exploded inside me.

"I don't care, Robert," I hissed, *"I'm ordering a small."*

Pete chuckled. "Really getting into that role, eh Lena?"

I glared at him, but then the waiter was there.

"One small, double cheese, double pepperoni," I barked.

I sat back while the others dithered about what toppings they wanted, now that they had to order one large. The waiter shifted from one foot to the other. At last they were ordering something, but their voices sounded far away. The lights seemed awfully bright, and as I lifted my hand to rub my eyes it felt like my hand had gained a few pounds since we walked in here. I put it down again. It lay there beside my cup of coffee, white and listless. In fact, it hardly seemed mine any more. The voices were growing even dimmer, and the table and the hand lying on it seemed to have detached themselves from me. I was somewhere up there on the wall, looking out on the scene.

Someone asked me a question. I don't know what it was. I tried to figure out who had spoken and what the words meant but I couldn't. Charmaine's hand came out and touched the hand on the table. They were all staring at me then. I thought I should say something but there were no more words in my head. They were all gone.

Suddenly there was pizza on the table.

There was a small one in front of me. I stared at it. It smelled great. Suddenly the hand moved. Another hand appeared on the other side of the plate. Somehow the hands picked up a slice of my double cheese, double pepperoni pizza and started shoving it into my mouth.

The first slice was down my throat in a minute. The second was mostly in my mouth when I noticed them all staring at me.

"What?" I said (or tried to say around all the pizza). "I'm hungry, okay?" At least the words were coming back.

"Yes, we can *see* that," said Robert with an arch look at Peter.

That was it. Suddenly I hated him more than I had ever hated anyone in my life.

I stood up, grabbed the side of their pizza that was nearest to me, and flung some of the slices at his smarmy little face. Charmaine screamed as her cup of coffee got caught on my sleeve and spilled all down the front of her sweat-shirt.

I sat down and finished chewing my pizza. I swallowed. I picked up the third slice and looked across at Robert.

He was sitting there stunned. There were little bits of ham and pineapple and green pepper stuck in his wavy black hair, and a thread of greasy cheese hanging from his chin. Beside him, Peter was wiping tomato sauce off his nose and trying not to laugh. Charmaine had stopped screaming and was moaning, "It's ruined, it's ruined!"

She looked up at me, horrified.

Our eyes met, and suddenly something crumpled up inside me. I burst into tears.

I just sobbed and sobbed. I sat for ages crying on what was left of my pizza. I couldn't move and I couldn't help it. Everything had turned out wrong, wrong, wrong.

Someone was beside me. There was an arm around my shoulder, a low, soothing voice.

"I know the signs," the voice was saying. "My sister has this. This is exactly what happens to her if she doesn't eat at the right time. Don't worry. Just eat your pizza. Just eat, eat . . ."

I finally figured out that it was Pete beside me. Somehow I managed to take a deep breath and stop sobbing. Someone (Charmaine, I think) put a few dozen napkins in my hand and I wiped my face and blew my nose and tried to look at her and Robert.

"I'm sorry, I'm so sorry," I said, over and over.

"Never mind, Lena," said Pete's voice. He picked up a slice of pizza and steered it toward my mouth. "Just eat, and you'll feel better soon. I personally guarantee it."

I ate. The waiter came with a cloth for the spilled coffee and Charmaine went away to the washroom, I guess to try to wipe off her sweat-shirt. Robert sat looking sullen and wounded, eating what was left of their pizza, looking anywhere but at me.

By the time everything was cleaned up I had finished my whole pizza. The lights weren't so bright. The voices weren't so far away. Pete was still beside me, munching on one of the slices that had survived my moment of madness.

I turned and looked at him. "Thank you."

He smiled at me, at *me* and no one else. "It's probably what my sister has – low blood sugar.

If you go too long without eating, your brain sort of shuts down and you go a bit crazy. You should see the doctor about it."

Charmaine was back, looking a little more coffee-coloured than she had when we came in. She picked up a soggy slice of pizza and frowned at me. But she looked more worried than mad.

"I'm okay, Char, really," I said to her. "I'll buy you a new sweat-shirt. I'm really, really sorry."

She waved a hand. "Forget it."

"Robert, I'm sorry. I didn't mean it. It wasn't the real me."

"Hmmph," he said, not looking at me.

"And I still want to be in the play. I still want to be Lady Bracknell."

"Of course you will be!" said Charmaine.

"Hmmph!" said Robert, a little louder.

So that's what happened. I couldn't believe I had actually thrown pizza at Robert. But I am still in the play; Robert muttered something about it being too late to recast my part anyway.

It didn't turn out all bad. Pete phoned me – actually *phoned me* – later that night and told me all about what he thinks I have. And he told me not to worry about Robert.

"He had it coming to him," he chuckled. "Anyways, we've got to keep you around for awhile. Only Lady Bracknell could've gotten away with a move like that."

I have to admit I've grown quite attached to the old bag.

Pete probably still likes Charmaine as much as ever. And he'll probably never ask me out.

But at least I got his attention.

THE TULPA

Eileen Kernaghan

The path rose before him, root-buttressed like a staircase, perilously steep. With the last of his strength Sangay scrambled to the top and found himself at the edge of a high, stony meadow. Beyond, to the northwest, rose lofty snow-peaks, glittering in the midday light.

It was a wild, lonely place, with not so much as a prayer-flag to mark a travelled path. But then, far across the tableland, Sangay glimpsed a solitary, swiftly moving figure.

The runner approached with a peculiar bounding gait, barely touching the earth with the balls of his feet, then springing high into the air like a bird unfurling its wings. Some distance past Sangay he glided to a halt and raised one hand in greeting, then beckoned to Sangay to catch up.

"May you be peaceful," said the runner. Sangay realized, suddenly, that this odd stranger was a woman. It was easy to see why he had been mistaken. She was very tall, even for a man; broad-shouldered, long-limbed, with the proud, erect bearing of a warrior-monk. Her eyes, set slantwise in a lean, sharp-angled face, were black as the shadows at the bottoms of ravines. Her hair seemed at one time to have been plaited, but it had long since escaped and now hung to her waist in a wild, black, tangled mass. She had chopped it in a ragged fringe across her brow and over it wore a peculiar hat of felted yak hair, with five points that stuck out round her head like tails. From a chain at her waist hung various charms and amulets, a number of small skin pouches, cooking pots in several sizes, and a magic knife, a *phurba,* in a fine embroidered case. A wolf-skin cape was tossed jauntily over one shoulder; beneath it Sangay glimpsed a shirt of soiled yellow silk and a dark red jerkin. Around her calves clung a long, limp skirt that might once have been white but was now an indeterminate shade of grey; beneath that were skin leggings and a ragged pair of embroidered boots.

"Well?" said the woman irritably, "have cannibal-demons eaten your tongue? Where do you come from, Little Monk, and where are you going?"

Not so little, he thought indignantly; he would soon be sixteen – a man, by anyone's reckoning.

He said, with dignity, "I am a monk of the White Leopard Monastery. I am seeking my path."

She gave a hoot of laughter. "A lost pilgrim – well, to be sure, there are plenty of those wandering the hills. Sooner or later the wolves get them." Her voice was low-pitched – more like a man's voice than a woman's – with a kind of rasp in it, like a gate hinge that has not been oiled for a long time.

"I have destination," Sangay assured her. "But now I must discover the true path that leads there."

She grinned. "Well then, for all you know your feet may be set upon it . . . Shall I come with you, Little Monk?"

He looked up at her in surprise – and then realized how fiercely he had hungered for companionship.

"How shall I keep pace with you? You must be trained in magic, to travel so fast."

She shrugged one fur-clad shoulder. "So? I run with the wind when it suits me. This morning it suited me. Maybe now it suits me to stump along at your side like a three-legged dog."

Sangay laughed in spite of himself. "And what shall I call you?"

"Jatsang," said the woman, grinning good-naturedly under her ragged fringe of hair. She turned, and without looking to see whether Sangay followed, set out at a brisk lope across the plain.

Late in the day they passed through a long, narrow gorge. Ahead lay a jumble of mountains – black snow-streaked cliffs and massifs heaped against a sunless sky.

Suddenly Jatsang put her finger to her lips in warning. Above the restless whining of the wind Sangay could hear the faint jangle of harness-bells. A moment later three men on tall black horses clattered into view.

They were dressed in tiger-skin robes and gaudy vests of embroidered silk, emerald green and garnet red. From under fox-fur hats their long glossy hair flowed down their backs. At their sides were swords encased in jewelled sheaths.

"Mind what you do," Jatsang hissed in his ear. "They are robbers, brigands. They will slit your throat from ear to ear and toss you to the wolves."

"Well met, sister," said the tall man who rode in front. His eyes were like river stones in his lean, rapacious face. "And you, Little Monk – what is your business here?"

Jatsang answered for them both. "We are *arjopas*, pilgrims."

"And I see the begging has been good," said the brigand. Smiling, he unsheathed his sword, and with one quick movement slashed straight across the bulge of Sangay's robe.

Sangay looked down at his last few cakes of tea, his string of cheeses, his bag of barley-meal, lying scattered in the dust.

"Pick them up," the robber-lord said mildly. "And hand them over." He reached out a leather-gloved hand.

With sinking heart Sangay watched his provisions disappearing into the robber-lord's saddle-bags.

"And the dagger," prompted the bandit, when Sangay had handed over the last cake of tea.

With that, Sangay's long habit of obedience vanished. He could not give up the beautiful dagger his family had given him.

"No," he said. He spoke softly – after years in the monastery, one always spoke softly – but no one hearing him could have doubted his determination.

"Give me the knife," said the robber. The point of his sword rested a scant inch from Sangay's breast.

Sangay's heart fluttered in his throat like a trapped bird, but he did not move. Thoughtfully the robber shifted his sword point upward, till it came to rest just under Sangay's chin. The dagger is precious, thought Sangay, as he felt the cold pressure of the blade against his throat – but is it worth dying for?

Slowly he drew the dagger from its belt and offered it to the bandit. With a wolfish smile the man closed his fingers on the beautiful gold-washed hilt. And at that moment the second robber rode down upon Jatsang.

In the midst of his horror and dismay, Sangay marvelled at Jatsang's serenity. Not so much as the twitch of a lip, the blink of an eye betrayed her as the robber's sword came up.

And then all at once there was something – a huge, unexpected, inexplicable something – towering up behind the bandit. One moment it was nothing more than the hint of a shape, a swirl of mist, a vague thickening of the thin grey air.

And the next moment it was real, and immense, and unequivocally flesh and blood – a knight, as tall as two ordinary men, as handsome as a god, looking down on the bandits with an expression not so much threatening as curious and eager.

He wore the rings of knighthood on his head and a long blue pleated robe the colour of the evening sky. In his belt was a great sword of antique design and on his left arm a vast shield covered with rhinoceros skin. He reached out and with one deft movement twitched the bandit's sword in mid-stroke from his hand and threw it clattering down the mountainside. Leaning down from his great height he seized the two robber-lords by their silken scruffs, lifted them from their mounts and tossed them casually to the ground. Then he stood gazing at Jatsang, looking for all the world like an enormous, good-natured, obedient dog.

From somewhere behind Sangay came muffled moans and the nervous stamping of a horse.

"Give back what Duggur has taken," he heard one man say, "else this sorceress will send her curses after us." With a series of small thuds, the tea, the cheese, the barley meal and the golden-hilted dagger all landed at Sangay's feet. Then hooves pounded across the hard-packed earth, as the robbers rode off with their wounded comrade. Finally Sangay managed to sputter, "How can this be, Lady? One minute there was no one there, and the very next . . ."

"Have you never seen a *tulpa,* a mind-phantom, made? No, I suppose not – in the monastery they only teach you to make tea and butter-images."

"I have heard of such things," said Sangay, tilting back his head to admire the phantom knight.

"He *is* a fine fellow, is he not?" said Jatsang. "I have not managed anything so impressive since the night I drove off a pack of wolves with thirty fire-demons. But now I suppose I'd better send him away."

"Must you?" asked Sangay, mindful of the long journey ahead.

The tulpa looked hopefully at Jatsang. Had he been the noble dog he so much resembled, thought Sangay, his ears would have stood up, and his tail would have wagged.

"Well, perhaps not," said Jatsang, wavering. "Maybe for a day or so . . . We'll see. After all, it was no small task, inventing him."

Sangay gathered up his treasures, and they went on through the bleak, dead land, the tulpa plodding cheerfully behind them, a vast, benign, and strangely comforting presence.

That night the tulpa crept close to Jatsang's small fire, spreading his great hands over the flames to warm them, as he saw the others doing. He neither ate, nor drank, nor spoke. As Jatsang nodded in the fire's warmth, Sangay saw the tulpa's form grow vague and insubstantial, translucent almost, so that the dim outlines of bushes and rocks showed through flesh and bone. For a long time Sangay watched and waited, curious to see what would happen when the sorceress slept; but finally he fell asleep himself.

For three days they travelled along a windswept ridge. Above lay cold grey slabs of rock; below, a narrow alpine lake covered with a skin of ice. At these heights there was neither shelter nor wood for a fire. Sangay dozed fitfully, his bones aching from the cold. Curled up in her skin cloak, Jatsang slept on undisturbed. The tulpa lay beside her, snoring faintly. In sleep he did not vanish, but grew pale and nebulous, like clotted mist. There was no more human warmth in that great billowy shape than in a bank of summer clouds, but still Sangay took comfort from his presence.

On the third night they came to the end of the ridge and descended into fir woods. Sangay gathered arm-loads of dead branches for fuel, and broke off some of the lower limbs to make a bed. His spirits lifted, thinking how comfortably he would sleep that night.

At dawn, while Jatsang still slept, he rose and gathered a fresh stack of firewood.

"What are you planning to do with that?" asked Jatsang, mildly curious and half asleep, as she watched him bundle it up with a cord.

"Carry it on my back," said Sangay. "There's high ground ahead, and I mean to be warm for another night at least."

Jatsang made a noise somewhere between a groan and a yak's grunt, indicating her disgust. "It will weigh you down like a stone," she pointed out, "and you have trouble enough to keep up as it is."

"Think how much faster I will walk after a good night's sleep," said Sangay stubbornly.

Jatsang shrugged. "Give it to the tulpa to carry, then."

"But he is a knight," said Sangay, shocked.

Jatsang looked at him with amused contempt. "He is a tulpa," she said.

But Sangay shook his head. Phantom shape though he might be, the tulpa had the true look and bearing of a Hero-Knight. To treat such a being as a mere servant, a bearer of firewood, would be a disrespectful and unseemly act.

And so Sangay shouldered his burden himself, though – just as Jatsang had predicted – the weight of it slowed his steps on the steep parts of the path.

As for Jatsang, uphill, downhill were all the same to her; and perversely, it seemed, she had stepped up the pace. For all that he was mountain-born, Sangay found his chest growing tight in the high, thin air. Finally, as he began to lose ground, Jatsang turned and snarled at him, "In the name of all the vulture-headed ones, Sangay, you try my patience too much. Either throw that wood in the gorge, or let the tulpa carry it."

And so he surrendered his burden to the tulpa, who gave him a good-natured grin and tossed the bundle onto his shoulder as though it had no weight at all.

Sangay marched on with lightened steps, still thinking about the hot meal and the warm bed he would enjoy that night.

Towards evening they came to a great gorge spanned by a narrow, swaying bridge of bamboo poles. The farther side was hidden in mist, and a torrent of white water raged below. Jatsang stepped out cautiously with Sangay close behind, setting his feet down slowly and carefully on the ice-slick surface. He stepped off the far side of the bridge with a small sigh of relief; then realized that the tulpa, whom he had thought was close behind him, was nowhere to be seen. What could have become of him? Sangay peered anxiously through the mist. Surely this huge, brave warrior was not afraid of heights?

Then, as a gust of wind parted the fog-curtain, Sangay saw the tulpa. He was standing in the centre of the bridge, with his back turned to Sangay. He had unfastened the rope on Sangay's precious bundle of firewood, and slowly, deliberately, like a child absorbed in a favourite game, he was dropping the sticks one by one into the river below.

"Tulpa," shouted Sangay, in bafflement and helpless rage. Hearing his cry, Jatsang whirled round. The tulpa turned too, gazing at Sangay with malicious glee as he tossed the last piece of firewood into the abyss.

They had been travelling for many days, and as the country grew ever wilder and more strange, so too did the behaviour of the tulpa-knight. Where once he had followed them with a dog's docile obedience, now he slunk at their heels like a great, stalking cat, so that they were forever watching their backs. At times he fell so far behind they thought they had lost him; and yet in the narrowest places he seemed to take a malign delight in crowding them to the edge. In appearance, too, he had altered. Sangay saw with dismay how lean and scraggy he had become. The great, broad face, once so placid and sweet-natured, had a haggard look, and into the eyes there had crept a hint of something sly and manipulative.

"Jatsang," said Sangay in grief and bewilderment, "what is happening to the tulpa?"

Jatsang glanced back to make sure their troublesome companion was safely out of earshot.

"Alas, it's as my teacher warned me," she replied. "I did not heed him, for I imagined I was too strong, too clever. But as you see, Little Monk, the tulpa is no longer my creature. He has become a thing apart from me, possessed of his own will."

"But what will you do, Lady?"

"Do? Why, I suppose I will have to destroy him."

Sangay's heart sank. Do you destroy a faithful guard dog because he digs up your garden or eats your shoes? Sangay would have answered no – but he was not Jatsang.

"Please, Lady," said Sangay, "do not kill the tulpa. He acts out of thoughtlessness, like a child – maybe if we are patient, he will mend his ways."

"How long shall I wait?" asked Jatsang. "Shall I wait until he drops *me* over the cliff instead of the firewood? If he is set loose in the world, he'll be a danger to anyone who crosses his path."

It was as though the tulpa had heard those words, so quietly spoken. When they halted to eat their evening meal, high up on the mountainside on a rock ledge, the tulpa hovered over them, an annoying and unsettling presence. His expression was wheedling, cajoling, sly as a monkey's. He reached out a hand to grasp the hem of Jatsang's robe; roughly, she slapped it away.

"Where is the tea?" Jatsang wanted to know. She upturned her pouch, shaking out bits of dried-up cheese, crumbs of buckwheat cake, a few grimy grains of rice. Scowling, she peered into its empy depths. "Sangay?" she said accusingly.

"I have not touched your pack," he said. His voice, in his own ears, sounded shrill and defensive; the tulpa had set his nerves on edge. Jatsang looked at the tulpa, who returned her gaze with cheerful insolence. Mimicking her, he pretended to hold an imaginary pouch, and fumbled through the invisible contents with his great, splay-fingered hands.

"Accursed one," said Jatsang, in a voice so soft that Sangay could barely make out the words, "what have you done with our tea?"

The tulpa rose and strolled to the edge of the precipice. Gleefully, he pointed into the yawning gulf below.

An awful silence followed. Sangay held his breath, waiting to see what would happen next. Jatsang's face was white with fury, but all she said to the tulpa, in a curiously flat, indifferent voice, was, "I am sick of the sight of you, tulpa. Go sleep behind those rocks, where we do not have to look at you."

Instead of obeying, the tulpa moved deliberately closer to the fire. Jatsang ignored him, and Sangay knew that the decision had been made. From now on, she would simply bide her time. After a while, like a bored child, the tulpa began to scoop up handfuls of small stones and toss them into the air. Tiring of that game, he threw one at Jatsang, hard enough to sting, and barely missed her head.

Clearly, the time had come. "Go," said Jatsang to the tulpa, her voice low and furious.

"You are banished from this world. I have no more need of you."

The tulpa got heavily to its feet. What a clumsy, shambling creature it had become, thought Sangay, when once it had been a thing of grace and dignity. Where now was the noble friend, the brave protector who had snatched him from the brigand's sword? Heartsick and without hope, Sangay offered up one final plea. "Maybe we do not need him now, Lady, but think of the journey that lies ahead . . ."

"For what will we need him?" Jatsang snapped. "To tramp through the fire, and wreck our belongings, and ruin our firewood, and split our heads with rocks? We can manage well enough without him, Little Monk. This is a demon I have called up, and I will be rid of him."

The tulpa stared sullenly at Jatsang, defying her. And then slowly he began to walk towards her – stiff-jointed, swaying, like a great wooden temple-image imbued with unholy life.

"Back, back," Jatsang hissed. Her jaw was clenched so hard that all the cords in her neck stood out. She began to curse the tulpa, a furious gust of words streaming from her lips. She leaped and whirled, stamping her feet hard on the ground at every turn as though she were crushing the tulpa's head beneath her heels.

She hurled more curses, spells of banishment, mystic syllables, exorcisms. All the while the tulpa – insolent, unmoved, immovable – went on staring at her with cold inhuman eyes. Finally, in her fury, Jatsang raised her hands and in a low, terrible voice she spoke a last dreadful incantation. Sangay felt a great blast of icy wind howl down across the plateau. So suddenly did it descend, and with such unexpected force, that Sangay was nearly blown off his feet. Staggering to regain his balance and pressing himself against the cliff-face, Sangay saw that the wind had caught the tulpa and lifted him up like a great air-filled bladder. Now it was sweeping him irresistibly towards the edge of the precipice. Over he went at last, tossing and swaying like some monstrous kite, drifting and turning in that vast grey gulf of air.

The wind buffeted the tulpa, tore at his hair and garments, rasped at him with sand and grit scoured up from the empty mountain-tops. And finally, in its frenzy, it ripped head from shoulders, limbs from body, flesh from bone. Tattered scraps of the tulpa, whipped and tossed like prayer-flags, hung for an instant in the icy air; and then they dissipated.

Jatsang sighed and shivered a little. With the slow stiff movements of exhaustion, she turned back to the fire.

"We are rid of him at last," she said. "He will not return."

In her voice there was neither relief nor satisfaction – only a sorrowing acceptance. Moved by comradeship, and his own grief, and a sudden unexpected pity, Sangay crept closer to her side.

"May you be happy," he whispered. "May you be peaceful. May you be free from pain." They were the words he would have spoken to a fellow monk – the only words of comfort he could find.

Jatsang gazed down at him. Her face seemed gentler, younger, in that flickering light. "Tell me, Little Monk," she said, "he *was* a fine tulpa, was he not? Better even than the thirty fire-demons . . ."

"Yes," said Sangay, sadly. "Surely better even than those."

Jatsang gave him a wry smile. Then she yawned, and stretched until all her joints cracked, and threw another juniper branch onto the flames.

LAURA

Gwen Davies

It is very dark when Laura's father gears the Volkswagen down to third, finally to second on the tiny road. The van seems to be going straight up. Out the window, wet snow lines the roadside. Beyond the snow, black evergreens patched with white make walls on both sides. "We are going to stay at a hotel," Laura whispers to those who listen in the dark.

The room is beautiful, green carpets like a forest floor, high brass beds, candelabra. Laura goes in alone and quietly closes the door.

"Welcome, Laura," the voice says. "Come."

She walks towards a large opening that appears in the far wall. It leads to a broad, shining pathway above the ground. The pathway is for

Laura to follow. She will be walking on air. At the end of the pathway, Laura can see in the distance that a red ladder leads up to a bright, round spaceship hovering above. Laura steps through the opening beyond the room.

"Look at that, those snow drops are out even before the snow's gone," says her father. Laura leans forward. The yellow headlights show tiny, snow-laden flowers bending on strangely green stems, poking above the snow.

"Sit down," her father says.

"I'm just trying to see."

"You can see from your seat."

Laura sits down quickly beford her father's hand can swing around to sting her. Not the fan of yellow lighting up the road tunnel, Laura can't see that from her seat. Her sister Peggy hasn't moved.

Finally, there are lights ahead. Then, a wide sweep of palace, grey stone in the street lights. Behind the palace the evergreen mountain rises into black night.

They park around the side of the building. Her mother hands Laura the plaid bag – the food bag – after tucking a coat over the open top. Laura feels ashamed to take food into this palace, into a hotel room. She takes her red plaid suitcase in the other hand and stays close to her mother, wishing she could not be seen. Peggy carries her own little brown suitcase, scuffed from long use.

Inside the lobby there are cherubs of pale stone flying over little fountains. Along the sides, the floor is covered by carpet deep as grass in royal blue. Above, chandeliers hang long and sparkling down into the room. Then, at the back, past the curving staircases, Laura sees glass-paned doors. Barely, breathlessly, she sees in the moonlight beyond a black lake bounded on three sides by the evergreen, silhouette forest.

"Take your bags, Laura, we're going to our room," her mother says. Going to their room to sneak supper. Here. To leave supper crumbs on the deep, soft carpets. She knows better than to ask if they can please, just this once, go to the dining room, be grand. Bad enough that it snowed and they had to go to a hotel instead of camping.

The silverware glistens, reflecting the crystal of the chandeliers. Waiters in black-tailed suits seat the family around a walnut table with white linen. The sounds of dishes and laughter, of bottles opening and orders being placed, are muted in the velvet drapes, the tapestry seats of the chairs – smooth, dark wood – chairs like the one Laura is sitting on to eat her dinner. The waiter is beside her, bowing, smiling at her . . .

"Laura, I'm not going to ask you again."

"What, Mom? I didn't hear you."

"Put the cloth out on the dresser and get out the dishes. Honestly, child."

"Where's Dad?"

"He went down to pay for the room."

"Can I go look around?"

"You can have your supper, and then we'll see what time it is."

Laura and her sister have the bed under the window. Peggy, sitting on the edge of the bed, flops down on her back and disappears into the soft covers. She giggles. Laura jumps after her.

"Don't jump on the bed," her mother says.

"Look at it. Peggy disappeared. Oh, it's like sleeping in a cloud."

"I want to sleep beside the window," Peggy says, crawling like a puppy in long grass around the bed.

"Take your shoes off, Peggy," Laura says. Peggy looks at her mother, at Laura, then takes her shoes off. The door opens and their father comes in.

"You girls stop bouncing on the bed," he says.

"Laura, put the plate of sandwiches out. Then both of you go and wash your hands," her mother says.

There is a sink in one corner of the room. It's made of marble with a leaf design on the taps. The gold is worn off the handles. There is only cold water.

"It's too cold," Peggy says.

"Just wash your hands and stop whining," says her father.

Laura suddenly realizes that she has never seen her parents wash their hands before a meal. They must get dirty. Money is dirty – she remembers her father saying that once when Peggy put a penny in her mouth. He was just paying for the room; he must have been touching money. She says nothing.

She is standing in the lobby of the hotel, looking at the cherubs and fountains and chandeliers. Her feet are drawn with a power she can't explain. She begins to climb one of the sweeping staircases. At the top is a dark red door which, as Laura approaches it, begins to open.

The room is bare inside, but it seems to glow. There is a faint hum, which grows louder. Then a voice says quietly, "Laura, it is time." She moves to the middle of the room. The floor begins to rise.

"Have you girls had enough?" her mother asks.

Laura looks at her empty plate. She doesn't feel hungry. She nods.

It is too late to go exploring after the supper things are put away. Laura and Peggy brush their teeth and then snuggle into bed. Laura is on the side away from the window closer to the door, feeling the covers hold her body, softly, all around. She loves the feeling. She can see out the window, the dark night with the tops of black evergreens pointing into the sky.

"Is Peggy asleep?" her mother asks quietly. Laura looks over at her sister, only a small face peeking out. She nods. "We're going downstairs for a bit. You go to sleep. We'll lock the door, you'll be all right. Nighty-night."

She talks like I'm two, Laura thinks. Now they'll go and do what they want to do. They'll dance and have some drinks. I don't even get to look around. Tomorrow we'll leave before breakfast – that's what Mom said. I want to see the lake. I want to see everything here. The door locks.

Laura goes to the glass-paned doors. On the handles are curved gold latches, just as she thought. She opens both doors and walks from the chandelier light out into the moon shadows across the stone terrace.

The lake glitters darkly. She begins to walk around it, towards the black forest side. The air is cool but Laura is not cold. Her slippers slide over the snow like skating. A voice in the night welcomes her. "We have been expecting you," it says. The voice is metallic.

A path opens before her. Slowly, the night around the path lightens as Laura walks. She comes to a clearing.

In it is a round spaceship which hovers above the ground, silently. From its centre, a red ladder extends to the ground. "Enter, Laura," the voice says. She reaches the ladder, places one hand on it, then realizes she can climb it like stairs. Above her the light is blinding. She will be leaving shortly.

Peggy's arm flops across Laura's chest. She moves over, closer to the edge of the bed. This always happens when she has to share a bed with her sister. Peggy flops and wiggles around in her sleep over the whole bed. Laura ends up balancing on the edge, trying to have a little space to herself. "Bed hog," she whispers. "You asleep?" she asks in a louder voice. There is no answer.

The moon has come out, a pale glow through the clouds on one side of the window. If she looked out the window, Laura could see the mountain and the forest. She could see the palace in the moonlight.

The windows are the kind that open like double doors. Moving slowly, Laura edges out from the warm, soft bed. She stands, watching through the window as the glow of the moon darkens. Her bare feet sink, even into the more worn carpet of the room, as she steps towards the window. She can see out as she rises to her highest tiptoes, holding the window ledge.

They are not on the lake side. It's even hard to tell they are on a mountain; the trees grow close around the palace and beyond the trees it is black dark. The moon has gone in and it's snowing again, huge, fluffy flakes that make Laura think of Christmas.

She pulls over a chair and, standing on it, opens the windows. After a while, she climbs up and sits on the sill. With her bare toes, she catches soft snowflakes that disappear when they touch. The cold makes her shiver.

The snow stops. The moon suddenly rides out from a cloud, making a soft rainbow around itself. "I really want to be the first woman on the moon," Laura says quietly. "I could see these mountains but they would look different from there. They would look like moon mountains look from the earth. I wonder if they would look like a face. I want to be a good astronaut. I will be a very good one. I will be the astronaut who flies the ship."

The moon dims, then the darkness comes back. There is nothing beyond the trees. Only Laura, the trees and the snow. Laura looks down the stone wall to the ground. They are on the first floor. It's still a long way to the ground.

She can feel the cold snow around her feet and ankles, but she is strong and it doesn't bother her. A path opens in the trees as she walks. She is drawn towards it, and though the path is dark, she realizes she can see.

Before her, then, is a light, growing brighter as she walks. There is a large clearing. In it, Laura sees – she gasps – a huge, round, saucer-shaped spacecraft. A red ladder goes from the ground to the centre of the ship. Laura feels herself pulled – it's like a voice, inviting her, reaching out for her . . .

She hears the sound of a key in the door. Her blood is suddenly cold in her chest. She must get into bed. But she has to go all the way around the bed, and the window is open, the chair is standing there. She is flying, she is under the covers.

It takes a moment before her parents see the open window. Then they see Laura, who stands frozen to the place where she landed beside the chair. "What are you doing out of bed?" her father asks. Laura says nothing.

"What are you doing?" He is coming towards her. "I put you in your bed to go to sleep. Why is the window open?" He takes her arm.

"Talk to me, damn it, what were you doing?"

Laura can't speak. There are too many things to say, and he's shaking her. He raises his hand. Laura feels herself shrink. She can feel the hot sting on her backside.

"No!" she yells. Then her voice just comes out. "Stop! Don't touch me! Let me go!"

He stops. Laura can't breathe, she is waiting, numb.

Nothing.

She feels the blood flush through the place on her arm where her father's hand has now let go.

Her walking feels stiff, she can hardly move. She can't look up, and has to be careful not to bump into anything. She lifts the covers. Feels the bed around her. The covers over her. Over her head. Her heart, her breath slow down, slow down. The bed feels so soft. Peggy's breathing is quiet beside her as she pulls the covers away from her nose, just so she can breathe.

She is walking down the path by the lake into the forest. Her slippers glide easily over the snow.

"Welcome, Laura," says the metallic voice. "We have been expecting you."

"I have come," says Laura.

The clearing opens before her. The ship, hovering in the centre, is glowing, humming quietly. The red ladder is down. Laura steps onto it. She finds she can climb it without holding on. As she ascends, the glow becomes brighter.

She steps into a large room. There are people of all ages. The ladder folds up and the ship closes over with a hush. A woman in white, with black hair and dark eyes, steps toward Laura. Slowly, evenly, the ship rises.

NOTES

HEATHER HAAS BARCLAY was born in Wimbledon, England and now lives in London, Ontario. She works as a volunteer with a women's correctional facility, as well as raising two children and writing. Her children's mini-novel *Miss Camilla Groundwater's Houseboat* was published in the *Canadian Children's Annual.* She has also published two novels for adults, *Buffett before Nightfall* and *Blues for Joy.*
RECOMMENDS: *The Happy Prince and Other Stories* by Oscar Wilde.

GWEN DAVIES was born in Port Colborne, Ontario and now lives in Halifax, Nova Scotia. She has published many articles and co-authored *Making Links: Developing Literacy Networks in Canada* (1990). Her career as a fiction writer began with the publication of a story in *The Pottersfield Portfolio* in 1990. This is her second fiction publication.
RECOMMENDS: *The Haunting of Frances Rain* by Margaret Buffie.

JOANNE FINDON was born in Surrey, B.C. and now lives in Toronto, where she is pursuing a Ph.D. in medieval studies. Her "Dragons at Mooncastle" was published in the *Canadian Children's Annual* (1988) and reprinted in Prentice-Hall's anthology *Cycles 1.*
RECOMMENDS: *A Darker Magic* by Michael Bedard.

JUDITH FREEMAN was born in Medicine Hat, Alberta and now lives in Ottawa, Ontario. She studied journalism at Carleton University and worked as a reporter for the *Calgary Herald*, Victoria *Daily Times* and Ottawa *Journal*. "Targets" is the first piece of fiction she has published.

ANN GOLDRING was born in Barrie, Ontario. She has taught senior English and studied creative writing at York University. Ann is an ardent environmentalist who published a pamphlet on composting in the 70s.
RECOMMENDS: *Covered Bridge* by Brian Doyle.

JAY HENDERSON was born in Dodsland, Saskatchewan and now lives in Cochrane, Alberta. He teaches in Calgary and acts as a teacher-consultant with the Calgary Writing Project. He has published poetry and a radio play, and has contributed numerous articles to The Totally Kids Page of the *Calgary Herald*.
RECOMMENDS: *The Last Wolf of Ireland* by Elona Malterre.

LINDA HOLEMAN was born in Winnipeg and has made her home there with her husband and three children. She holds a Master's in Educational Psychology from the University of Manitoba and taught for two years in an isolated native community in Manitoba. She has been reviewing material for the journal of the Canadian Library Association, *Canadian Materials*, since 1989, and has had her own work published in a number of

magazines. Currently she is "working on" literary publications.
RECOMMENDS: *Two Moons in August* by Martha Brooks.

JULIE JOHNSTON was born in Smiths Falls, Ontario and now lives in Peterborough, Ontario. She is a full-time author of award-winning plays, numerous short stories and articles. *Hero of Lesser Causes,* a full-length prose work, was published by Lester Publishing this year.
RECOMMENDS: *A Long Way from Verona* by Jane Gardam.

EILEEN KERNAGHAN was born in Enderby, B.C. and now lives in Burnaby. She and her husband own Neville Books. Eileen has published award-winning fantasy stories and novels. Her titles include *Journey to Aprilioth* (1980) and *Songs from the Drowned Lands* (1983). In 1990 she published a non-fiction work, *Walking after Midnight.*
RECOMMENDS: *Tulku* by Peter Dickinson.

MICHAEL KILPATRICK was born in Geraldton, Ontario and now lives in Toronto. He is a former journalist and columnist who teaches at George Brown College. He has contributed to CBC Radio's "Matinee" and "The Inside Track".
RECOMMENDS: *Ordinary People* by Judith Guest.

JEAN RAND MacEWEN lives in Toronto, where she was born. She is a former teacher who has been active in the areas of special education and creative writing. As well, Jean is an avid puppeteer who presented shows for children using hand puppets and marionettes.

R.P. MacINTYRE lives in Saskatoon, Saskatchewan, where he was born. A full-time writer and dramatist and sometime actor, he has worked with students in the schools as well as with the media. In 1985 his "Toy Boat" script won the Saskatchewan Showcase Film and Video Best Drama Award. In 1991 he published the young adult novel *Yuletide Blues* with Thistledown Press.

SHARON GIBSON PALERMO was born in Philadelphia, Pennsylvania, studied in Boston, and settled in Halifax, Nova Scotia with her Canadian husband. She holds two Master's degrees in Education and has been teaching at pre-school and elementary levels for twenty years. Her fiction for children has won several prizes from the Writers' Federation of Nova Scotia, and in 1993 her first juvenile novel will be published by Nimbus.

JOCELYN SHIPLEY was born in London, Ontario and now lives in Newmarket, Ontario. She is the parent of three children who has found time to write poetry and to publish four non-fiction titles for children and their parents, including two titles on *Making Your Own Traditions.*
RECOMMENDS: The Isis Trilogy by Monica Hughes and Susan Cooper's fantasy series.

LOIS SIMMIE was born in Saskatchewan and has made her home in Saskatoon. She is the author of poetry, short stories and drama for children, including *Auntie's Knitting a Baby* and *Who Greased the Shoelaces?* She has also produced the short story collection *Pictures* and the very funny novel *They Shouldn't Make You Promise That.*

JENNIFER TAYLOR was born in Hamilton, Ontario and now lives in Sooke, on Vancouver Island. She has written award-winning stories and has had material published in small magazines.
RECOMMENDS: *Howl's Moving Castle* by Diana Wynne Jones.

ANN WALSH was born in Jasper, Alabama and now lives in Williams Lake, B.C. In between she lived in South Africa, Kansas and finally Vancouver, where she earned an education degree at U.B.C. She is now involved with adult literacy and is active in many writer's organizations. She is the author of plays and novels for young people, including *Your Time, My Time*; *Moses, Me and Murder*; and *The Ghost of Soda Creek*, as well as books for big folks.

BUDGE WILSON was born in Halifax and lives in Hubbards, Nova Scotia. She is the mother of two daughters. She worked as a commercial artist, a free-lance photographer and a fitness instructor before starting to write. Her writing career has generated numerous short stories and novels, of which ten are for children and young adults. Her story collection *The Leaving* (Stoddart, 1990) has been a major popular and critical success.
RECOMMENDED: *The Leaving* and *Lorinda's Diary* by Budge Wilson.

JUDITH WRIGHT was raised in rural Saskatchewan and lives in Saskatoon. She has worked in professional theatre in Canada and Europe. Her shorter work has appeared in *Fireweed* and *Fiddlehead.* Her first young adult novel, *Magpie Summer,* was published by Polestar Books in 1992.
RECOMMENDS: *Bad Boy* by Diana Wieler.